The Belles of Desire, Mississippi

Book One

Ghosts of Summerleigh Series

By M.L. Bullock

Dedication

To all the little liars.

Haunted Houses

All houses wherein men have lived and died
Are haunted houses. Through the open doors
The harmless phantoms on their errands glide,
With feet that make no sound upon the floors.

We meet them at the doorway, on the stair,
Along the passages they come and go,
Impalpable impressions on the air,
A sense of something moving to and fro.

There are more guests at table, than the hosts
Invited; the illuminated hall
Is thronged with quiet, inoffensive ghosts,
As silent as the pictures on the wall.

The stranger at my fireside cannot see
The forms I see, nor hear the sounds I hear;
He but perceives what is; while unto me
All that has been is visible and clear.

We have no title-deeds to house or lands;
Owners and occupants of earlier dates
From graves forgotten stretch their dusty hands,
And hold in mortmain still their old estates.

The spirit-world around this world of sense
Floats like an atmosphere, and everywhere
Wafts through these earthly mists and vapors dense
A vital breath of more ethereal air.

Our little lives are kept in equipoise
By opposite attractions and desires;
The struggle of the instinct that enjoys,
And the more noble instinct that aspires.

These perturbations, this perpetual jar
Of earthly wants and aspirations high,
Come from the influence of an unseen star,
An undiscovered planet in our sky.

And as the moon from some dark gate of cloud
Throws o'er the sea a floating bridge of light,
Across whose trembling planks our fancies crowd
Into the realm of mystery and night,—

So from the world of spirits there descends
A bridge of light, connecting it with this,
O'er whose unsteady floor, that sways and bends,
Wander our thoughts above the dark abyss.

Henry Wadsworth Longfellow, 1807-1882

Prologue—Harper Belle

Desire, Mississippi
September 1942

Dressed in nothing but a cotton slip and a head full of rag rollers, I tiptoed to the rusty screen door. Poised impatiently with my hands on my skinny hips, I frowned at my sister's shadow as she crossed the front porch.

"Momma is going to kill you D-E-A-D, Jeopardy Belle! You better get in here before she finds out you've been out all night," I whispered disapprovingly at her silhouette as I reached up to unhook the screen door latch. My eyes felt like someone had thrown a handful of sand in them, but I could very clearly see my sister's petite frame and the outline of her long, wild hair.

Didn't she know I had gotten in late myself? Aunt Dot was sleeping in my room with me tonight. She'd been my chauffeur for the Harvest Dance. It had been the happiest night of my life, except for Jeopardy's absence.

I had to protect my sister from Momma's wrath. I had lain awake almost all night listening for the sound of her footsteps on the porch or her fingers tapping at my bedroom window. I'd just about given up hope that she would ever come home until at last I heard the creaking porch boards, the evidence of her late arrival. Maybe instead of covering for her, I should have told Momma or Aunt Dot everything— that Jeopardy went out smoking and drinking with whatever boy she took a fancy to just about every night of the week—but I couldn't do it. I could never bring myself to break her confidence. Doing so would mean I would abandon my role as the family peacemaker; I might have been a lot of things, but never disloyal, especially not to Jeopardy—she had so few friends. She needed me.

"Honestly, Jeopardy. I don't know why you have to be so stubborn," I whispered as I struggled with the latch. It didn't want to budge this morning for some strange reason. Daddy had installed it too high, so I had to stand on tiptoe to pop it open, but I finally got a good grip on it. Easing the door open slowly to avoid its obnoxious squeaking, I waited for Jeopardy to stumble inside. Once I smuggled her back into the house and up to her room, I was going to give her a real piece of my mind, and good too. Lightning popped across the dim morning sky; I expected it to illuminate Jeopardy's guilty face. How was it that she was the oldest? Not only was I the most mature of the Belle sisters, but I was also the tallest and the plainest. And this morning, I was certainly the most tired.

Was tiredest even a word? Thank goodness I didn't have school this morning, and thank goodness today wasn't the George County Spelling Bee. My brain was too sticky and exhausted to put two letters together, much less o-n-o-m-a-t-o-p-o-e-i-a. I couldn't abide it if Martha Havard won the spelling bee. I'd have to move to Mobile with some distant cousin just to escape the shame of it. Not that anyone in this house cared. Momma would show up for the

Harvest Queen competition but never the spelling bee.

Suddenly the bottom fell out of the sky and rain trickled through the leaks in the tin roof porch, but to my surprise, my older sister was nowhere to be found. I closed my eyes and opened them again, but she did not appear. I flipped up the hook and opened the screen door, completely puzzled by this turn of events. I had seen her—I had certainly seen her! Suddenly, my tummy felt like a bowl of spoiled jelly, all wiggly and uncertain.

Something was wrong. Was I dreaming? Had I fallen asleep?

"Jeopardy? Don't play games with me." I stepped onto the wet concrete of the screened-in porch, and even though it was predicted to be a scorcher of a day after the rain, my feet were freezing. It was as if I were standing nude in the soda shop, the only place in town with air conditioning, and every hair on my body stood at attention. An unholy cold crept into my bones. *Where could she be?* We had no back porch furniture except Momma's rocking chair, and a full-grown girl of fifteen couldn't hide behind it. Even one as petite as Jeopardy Belle.

This had to be some sort of joke. "Jep?" She hated that nickname, but seeing as she wanted to play games with me, I had no alternative but to insult her. I searched the porch and even the narrow stairs leading up to it, but there was no sign of Jeopardy. I knew I had heard her footsteps; I had even seen her figure a minute ago. No way could she move on and off the porch that quickly, especially not in the clunky white high heels she wore last night unless she had managed to lose them somewhere. I prayed that was not the case because they were probably Momma's. Jeopardy was particularly fond of them, and she was one to take risks. Momma would be fit to be tied if her favorite pair of heels came up missing. She'd had to send away to Montgomery Ward to get those shoes.

A voice from behind me surprised me. "Harper? What are you doing out here? It's raining cats and dogs. You'll catch your death. Are you walking in your sleep again?"

I had no choice but to lie to Momma. She and Jeopardy carried on a lifelong feud, and I was one to strive for peace, even if that meant lying to one or the other if need be. I would do as much for Jeopardy to make her think more highly of our Momma. In some ways, it was as if I were the grown-up in our family.

Where are you, Jeopardy Belle? Maybe I *had* been dreaming or sleepwalking. I used to do it all the time before we moved to Summerleigh.

"Sorry, Momma. I didn't mean to frighten you." To my surprise, she hugged me. Hugs were distributed infrequently in our home and were rarer than a ribeye steak dinner. I breathed her in, enjoying her particular fragrance of peaches and cold cream.

"Come inside and help me make biscuits. You girls have choir practice this morning." She kissed my cheek and patted my back as we walked into the house. I swallowed the lump in my throat and resisted the urge to spill my guts to Momma. Maybe if I knew she wouldn't unleash her rage on Jeopardy, I would have been more forthcoming. In hindsight, I would regret not telling her everything right then and there, but hindsight is always twenty-twenty, as they say.

I heard my youngest sister crying loudly enough to wake up the rest of the household. As Momma lit a slender cigarette and took a puff, I said, "I'll get Loxley, Momma. She's probably soaked through her clothing." Caring for Loxley would provide me enough of a distraction to gather my wits and come up with some sensible explanation for Jeopardy's absence.

My mother looked tired this morning. I clearly saw the fine lines around her mouth and between her eyes despite the thick layer of powder she had applied to her face. She wasn't even thirty-five, but she didn't smile much anymore. When was the last time I'd seen Momma smile? It sure wouldn't be this morning. "I don't know why Loxley has to wet the bed every night. You girls aren't giving her water at night, are you?"

"No, ma'am."

She frowned again. "She's five now, too old to leave puddles behind."

"Yes, ma'am," I agreed. "I will clean her right up." Maybe if I softened the blow with some good deeds, my mother wouldn't get crazy angry when she found out that her oldest daughter was nowhere to be found.

"No, I'll go tend to Loxley, dear. You start sifting the flour." My stomach did a double clutch as I watched her walk away. I hoped she wouldn't go up to Jeopardy's room and discover one Belle missing. Momma walked down the threadbare carpet runner toward the bedroom where Loxley and Addison slept. Jeopardy and I used to share the smaller room just beyond, but she usually slept in the attic of our dilapidated mansion now.

I dumped flour into the sifter and added the salt and baking powder. *Darn you, Jeopardy!* I thought as I tapped the flour through the sifter, pausing only a few seconds to light the gas stove. The stove was the only luxury in this big old house; Daddy had really come through for us with the new Wedgewood stove. It was a beauty and cranked up with just one strike of the match. *I miss you, Daddy!*

Daddy had been something of a dreamer, but you couldn't help but love him anyway. He was so handsome and kindhearted that even Momma loved him, even if most of the time his head was in the clouds. I heard Momma once tell her closest friend, Augustine Hogue, that even when Daddy wasn't away at war, he was there in his mind. War does things to people's minds. Or at least that's what everyone says. *I wonder if Loxley is right. Does Daddy haunt this place?* When he was away on the battlefield, he rarely wrote; he always promised to write but never did. And now Jeopardy was missing.

Oh, Daddy. What do I do?

Reaching for the biscuit pan, I greased it with a faded checkered kitchen rag and set about finishing up the biscuits. Loxley must have made a real mess because it was ages before I heard Momma again. At least Loxley wasn't crying anymore, which meant she hadn't been spanked for her accident this morning. That meant Momma was in a good mood. *How long would that last now?* Once the biscuits were in the oven, I started the coffee percolator going and took the peach jelly and butter out of the refrigerator. The phone rang, and Momma answered it and put a pouting Loxley in the chair beside her. It was Augustine Hogue calling to share the news that there was a new opening at the church. From what I could hear of the conversation, Reverend Reed needed a new secretary now that Ola got married, and there was going to be quite a bit of interest in the position. Even Momma thought it might be nice to apply for the job.

I must have looked out the kitchen window a half dozen times, but there was no sign of Jeopardy. A bright September sun rose over the thick clump of peach trees in the backyard, and still nothing. It was late for the peach crop, but the trees continued to produce copious amounts of the succulent fruit. Any day now, Momma would send us girls up the trees again to collect peaches so we could sell them to our neighbors. Jeopardy had always been the best at climbing. *Where are you, sister?* I supposed in some homes it would've been strange to have a child missing for breakfast. But that's how things were around here.

Sometimes Momma and Jeopardy went days without speaking or even looking at one another. I didn't understand it at all, but I had to believe they loved each other. I kept my silence during breakfast, and thankfully Momma didn't ask about the missing Belle. Loxley chomped on her food, and Addison picked at hers but ate a few bites while Momma finished her phone call. She and Miss Augustine made quite a meal of Ola and Reverend Reed. I guess they'd closed their ears during the pastor's latest sermon about gossip and the dangers of "wagging tongues." Despite the evils of gossip, I was glad that Momma had something to distract her from Jeopardy's latest escapades.

"Girls, get dressed for practice. I'll tidy up here, and Harper can walk you down to the church. I guess your sister doesn't plan on participating?" Momma arched an eyebrow at me over her chipped coffee cup, and I stumbled over an answer. Nothing sprang to mind, and my stomach churned as if at any moment it would reject the few crumbs of biscuit I'd eaten and the glass of milk I'd swallowed. I was no good at lying, and knew I would fail miserably at any attempt. I knew I should have woken up Aunt Dot. She would know how to soften the blow.

I am going to fail you, Jeopardy. I can't do it, I thought as tears filled my eyes. Before I could open my mouth and confess my sister's sins, someone banged like a freight train on the screen door. Startled at such an early caller, we all trailed behind

Momma as she went to answer it, and she didn't shoo us away. Unlike me, she didn't have a head full of rag rollers but looked pretty as a picture, complete with a neat dress and perfect makeup.

To our surprise, the caller was Deputy Andrew Hayes. I couldn't help but smile at him. He was almost as handsome as Daddy with his short brown hair, serious eyes and tidily pressed uniform. He spoke to Momma in low, serious tones, but I couldn't hear a word he said. He clutched Jeopardy's purse in his hands, along with Momma's stolen high heels. Momma's white hand clutched the doorframe as she listened to the deputy. Another vehicle pulled into the driveway at a high rate of speed. It kicked up dust and rocks, and Loxley began to cry. All I could hear was the beating of my own heart. Something bad had happened to Jeopardy. Something really bad.

This can't be right! I saw her this morning—she was just here! Momma turned around with Jeopardy's things in her hands. Her blue eyes searched mine and her lips moved, but I couldn't hear her either.

Suddenly I heard something heavy hit the ground beside me, and then the world went black.

Chapter One—Jerica Poole

A year ago, my alarm clock was much sweeter than the one that screamed at me this morning. *Marisol, I miss you, sweetheart.* I missed being awakened by butterfly kisses and warm arms around my neck, and to add to my agony it had been another dreamless night. After I beat the buzzing alarm clock half to death, I reached for my daughter's picture. Forever frozen in time, Marisol smiled back at me, showing her missing front tooth and a sprinkling of freckles across her nose. I kissed the dusty glass and whispered, "Another day, baby girl."

I took my time getting out of bed and knew without turning over that I was alone—again. Eddie showed up last night, and like a fool, I let him in. One moment of weakness. That was all it took to welcome chaos back into my life...but I'd been so alone lately, and Marisol's sixth birthday had come and gone. Eddie and I had shared a silent meal, avoiding talking about Marisol, and then made love, but it was an empty coupling without healing or emotions. It was not as it once was. I tried to remember that he was also a broken person, that he had also lost a child. He did not make it easy for me to have sympathy for him because as usual, sometime last night or early this morning, Eddie had left me. I had smartly hidden my purse in the cedar chest before our dinner together, but I had completely forgotten about hiding the contents of my medicine cabinet. The chances were good that my ex-husband had relieved me of my anxiety and depression prescriptions.

Please, God. Cut me a break.

Placing Marisol's picture back on the nightstand, I pulled on my robe. Rain slapped the side of the house—the weatherman had gotten it right for once. He'd warned the residents of Portsmouth, Virginia, that it was going to rain all day. *Yeah, that rain sounded ferocious, like BBs striking the windows.* I had first shift today, and I couldn't miss another day of work. I'd burned up my sick days with various personal appointments with therapists, wellness checkups—you name it. Nothing helped, nothing diminished my grief. I lost myself in an endless cycle of work, hence the ever-expanding collection of medications. It was better to pretend I did not feel than to actually experience the agony of my loss on a daily basis.

Might as well face reality.

I faced the mirror of the medicine cabinet and stuck my tongue out at myself. Why in the world had I let Eddie into my home, and how had he found me? Before this most recent hookup, I hadn't seen him for six months. I opened the cabinet, and sure enough, my meds were gone.

"Damn it, Ed!" I closed the cabinet and dug my purse out of the cedar chest. It didn't take long to figure out that he'd discovered my hiding spot. Everything was out of place, but at least he'd left my credit cards and checkbook alone. All my cash had disappeared. "Eddie! You bastard," I said under my breath. I couldn't have predicted that he would stoop that low, but his pill addiction apparently had a hold on him. *If you'll rob a grieving mother, your own ex-wife, of her cash and medication, you're pretty low-down.* "That's the last time, Eddie Poole. The last time!" I wiped a tear from my eye. I had a few groceries in the house, but I needed that cash for gas and my lunches all this week.

No sense in crying over spilled milk. That's something my grandmother used to say when she dealt with her son, my father. In other words, *It's too late to do anything about what's been done.* Yeah, that would have to be my motto too now. It was too late for Eddie and me. Our chances died along with Marisol.

I began my weekday morning ritual and prepared to face my day. I drank two cups of black coffee, got dressed in my pink uniform, smoothed back my hair in a bun and dabbed on a bit of makeup. Next, I put dinner in my mini crockpot: today's menu choice was a chicken breast, a can of chopped tomatoes and green chilies and half a can of black beans. I detested fast food but loved the salad bar at the restaurant near the nursing home. Unfortunately, I had no cash for lunch now. Unlike my ex, my crockpot never let me down. I turned the pot on low and grabbed my purse and umbrella. It was summer, so I didn't need a jacket, but a raincoat was obviously a necessity today. Luckily for me, I would be inside all day.

Count your blessings, as one of my therapists reminded me every week.

My car didn't want to start this morning, and I quickly forgot about counting my blessings when I finally coaxed the engine to turn over. Jetting down Twelfth Street, I pulled into the parking lot of the Sunrise Retirement Home. Since my shift began at 6 a.m., I had plenty of parking spots to choose from and I picked a close one. That was one of the advantages of coming in early. The night shift was basically a skeleton crew.

As administrative nurse and coordinator, I walked into any number of emergencies every Monday. What would it be this morning? I wondered if Mr. Munroe had made it through the weekend without a trip to the hospital. He really needed to go, but he refused to thus far. At least one of my favorites, Mrs. Nancy Grimes, had a visitor last Friday. The first in months. Sweet lady. She always had a joke to share.

But the one resident I hated leaving the most was Harper Hayes. Mrs. Hayes, who insisted I call her Harper, was a firecracker with a penchant for telling the honest truth—about everything. She and I became fast friends when I was pregnant with Marisol. In fact, my favorite resident of the Sunrise Retirement Home had given me an "All About Baby" book and showered my baby with gifts including a silver spoon, crocheted booties and a dedication gown. And when Marisol died, she'd cried alongside me. We were an odd family, the three of us. Yes, it was hard to leave her on the weekends, but she insisted on it. She reminded me that I needed to have a life outside this place. The truth was, I didn't have much of one. As last night had proved.

To my surprise, there had been absolutely no emergencies this weekend. None at all. I checked the boards twice for messages or notices, but there wasn't anything that required my attention. Nothing on my computer screen either. "Well, that's a change," I said to Anita, my right-hand nurse and work buddy. "No emergencies at all?"

She smiled, her dark skin glowing prettily. "Yeah, everyone was well behaved. Uh, you won't believe this, but Eddie's been calling this morning. He started calling a few minutes before you got here."

"He's got a lot of nerve. He's lucky I don't call the cops."

Anita tossed her pen on the desk in front of her and gave me an incredulous look. "Tell me you didn't. You went through all that to get moved, and then you let him in."

I buried my head in my hands and refused to meet her gaze. "I know. I'm a loser. This isn't an excuse, but I've been so lonely lately. I guess he just caught me at the right moment."

"More like the wrong moment. For someone with so much education, you sure do need your head examined." I accepted her gentle scolding, for I knew her heart.

"Believe me, it's been examined, and I don't think there's any hope for me."

One of the new nurses, Jenny, came to the desk and said, "There you are. Mrs. Hayes has been waiting for you, Jerica. She sent me to come find you and asked you to come see her at your earliest convenience."

It was my turn to raise my eyebrows in surprise. "And that's how she said it? That doesn't sound like Harper Hayes."

Jenny blushed and confessed, "She didn't say it exactly like that. I paraphrased for her."

"Oh, she's in one of those moods. I'm on the way. Thanks." I tucked my purse in the top drawer of my desk and headed down the hall to see my friend. I had barely stepped my foot in the door before she instructed me to come in.

"Thank goodness. I didn't think I would make it to Monday. Have a seat. I know you're busy, but I really need to speak with you." I joined Harper at the small table next to the window that overlooked the garden. I barely had the time to sit and visit with her during the day except during these early mornings.

"What are you talking about? Are you sick?" I frowned at her suspiciously. "You can't wait for me to be here to tell someone, Harper. What's the matter?"

"Hush now and listen. I have something to show you." She slipped a picture out from under a lace doily that topped her round table. "Look at us, Jeopardy."

"Jerica, I'm Jerica, Harper." My heart fell to hear her get my name wrong. Doing so once was forgetfulness, but she'd done it quite a bit recently and it worried me.

"Yes, I know that. Now take a look."

The black and white photo had crumpled, brittle edges, but the faces were clear. Four girls looked back at me, three with smiles and one with a faraway look as if she were seeing past the moment—as if she could see me. I shivered at the silliness of that thought.

"Can you guess which one is me?" She smiled like the Cheshire cat, and I stared at her and then at the photo. Picking out Harper was easy. You could tell the girls were related, but none of them looked exactly alike. Unwilling to wait for my answer, she said, "That's me, on the end."

I smiled at her. "You haven't changed a bit."

"Oh, you're such a liar, Jerica Poole, but thank you." Thank goodness she didn't call me Jeopardy again. But I wasn't lying. Of course, she looked much older than this photo, but it was Harper nonetheless. She had a wide forehead and neat eyebrows that had a natural arch to them. In the photo, she wore a Peter Pan blouse, and her soft blond hair was bobbed and curled.

"And which sister is which?"

"Now, this pouty thing with the bee-stung lips is my sister Addison. She's the only one of us who had brown eyes. She looked a lot like my father's family. Addison was a sickly girl but sweet." Addison had a cleft chin to go along with those full lips. She was certainly a pretty girl. "This ball of sunshine was my youngest sister, Loxley. Momma always braided her hair into two braids. She used to see ghosts all the time, right up until the day she moved away and married that boy from Mobile. Why can't I think of his name?"

"What?" I laughed at that. "Loxley must have had an imaginary friend or two, I gather?"

"No, they weren't imaginary friends; she saw ghosts just like you and I see cats or dogs. And this girl here, the one beside me, that's my sister Jeopardy. She disappeared in 1942." I was mesmerized by the girl with the wild blond hair. She looked so out of place, like a girl from another time had stepped into the frame. She wore a white sundress and had vulnerable-looking bare arms and that sad, faraway look in her eyes.

"She looks so tiny. She was the oldest, right?"

"Yeah, she was the oldest, but I was the tallest. I was the Ugly Duckling of the Belle family, taller than even Momma when I got older. Jeopardy was always a petite thing, with a wild streak a mile wide. Oh, how I wanted to be like Jeopardy." Harper clutched the photo in her hand and closed her eyes as if she were remembering some half-forgotten moment. I didn't want to interrupt her, but I was captivated by the photograph.

"Hardly an Ugly Duckling, Harper. And I'm taller than you. Tell me about your sisters. You said Jeopardy disappeared?"

"They are all gone now. I am the last Belle." She opened her eyes and tucked the crocheted blanket around her legs. "Chilly this morning. I wanted to see you, Jerica, because I am going to die soon, and I'm afraid I have failed to bring my sister home. I made a promise a long time ago. I promised Jeopardy I would bring her home, but I couldn't. I need your help. Please tell me you'll help me. I can't die knowing she'll never make it home."

Alarmed at her confession, I put my hand on her wrist to comfort her. "Hey, you aren't going to die on my watch. Let me call your doctor. If you feel off in any kind of way, we need to get him here."

"Don't do that. I need you to believe me. I can't explain how I know it, but I do—I am going to die soon, and I need your help. I can't find Jeopardy, and she's been gone so long. She can't rest until we find her. Please help me." For the first time in all the years I'd known her, Harper Hayes cried. I was so surprised that I couldn't imagine refusing her. I couldn't say no to her after she'd been so good to Marisol and me. She'd been there for me when I needed her most. I would have to return the favor.

"I'll help you, Harper, but we have to call Dr. Odom. I'll help you if you allow me to call him."

She wiped her tears away and nodded in agreement. "That sounds like a fair trade. Hand me my handkerchief, please."

I walked to her bedside table and retrieved one of the embroidered handkerchiefs from her neat stack. Handing it to her, I couldn't help but hug her even though I suspected she didn't enjoy hugs too much.

"I want you to have this picture, Jerica. I don't want you to forget Jeopardy Belle, not like everyone else has. Even me—I forgot her for a while. I tried to find her, but then I got so busy with my own life. Find her, Jerica. Find her and bring her home."

"I can't accept this picture, Harper. These are your sisters, not mine."

"No, I want you to have it. Just remember your promise. I'm going to hold you to it now, Jeopardy."

I didn't correct her but squeezed her hand and slipped the picture into my pocket before I walked out to call Dr. Odom. The whole thing was weird, but I couldn't refuse Harper. She'd been there for me, and how hard could it be to find her sister?

She disappeared in 1942...

Chapter Two—Harper Belle Hayes

Monday's child is full of grace...Nope. That's not how it goes.

"Mm-hmm," I answered the doctor absently as he poked and prodded me with his cold metal tools. I disliked doctors immensely, but I'd made Jerica a promise, and her promise would be harder to keep than mine. I had no doubt she could do it. Jerica had a quiet strength that would take her far if she could tap into it. So much like my Aunt Dot.

Tuesday's child will win the race. Uh-uh. That's not right either. How strange that Loxley had sung this in my dream last night and now I couldn't remember any of it. I used to know this song and about a dozen others by heart.

"Poke out your tongue, please," the young man said as he unceremoniously shoved a wooden tongue depressor in my mouth. *Good Lord! I don't have tonsillitis.* This silly doctor was messing up my concentration. It was easier to remember this poem when you sang it; we used to sing it, all us Belle girls together. Hard to sing with a Popsicle stick in your mouth. Jumping rope had been a happy pastime of ours; Jeopardy had always been the best at it, so much so that she got bored with it and went on to other things like boys and smoking, but the rest of us continued until we were all too big for the jump rope.

Dr. Odom mumbled something about potassium levels to Jerica, further proof that he was a fool. I didn't need a banana...I was dying. I knew this because Loxley told me; I saw my baby sister in a dream last night. And she had been as she always was, sweet-faced and wise beyond her years. Loxley had been Tuesday's child. *Full of grace...yes, I think that's right.* My eyes closed; I'd been so sleepy yesterday and today too. The next thing I knew, I was opening my eyes and back home. Back at Summerleigh, on the landing, in the full sunlight that shone through the big window. Loxley was there, her neat braids shiny and her blue checkered dress tidy for once. And in that moment, when I cleared the stairs at Summerleigh and ran to the end of the hallway to hug her, all the things that drove me crazy about her when we were young didn't matter anymore. I didn't care that she always lost her lunch money or that she peed the bed or had a habit of vomiting if she ate too much. I loved her beyond reckoning.

And Summerleigh...I had forgotten how magical the place had been when I was a child. I had loved it since the day I first clapped eyes on it. It had all seemed so rotten and broken, like a forsaken sand castle those first few days, but there was beauty there, beneath the rotten boards and peeling paint. Daddy never doubted the house's potential.

"Summerleigh is a prize worth having, and we'll work night and day if that's what it takes to restore her," he told us proudly. "I won this house fair and square—you should have seen my hand, Ann—and now we will keep it." Knowing Daddy, he totally believed this declaration. Momma didn't speak against the place after that, not in Daddy's hearing, anyway, but she sure didn't lift a finger to do any of the work required. Momma's hobbies were picking peaches, smoking her skinny cigarettes and talking on the phone. When Daddy was home, she did all the cooking. But if he was gone to take a load somewhere—he was an over-the-road truck driver after he left the military—I did it all. It was like she was Momma when Daddy was home, but when he was gone, I was the Momma. Funny how at the time it didn't seem strange to me. It was just life.

I remember her burning up the phone lines once the phone company managed to put one in the kitchen at Summerleigh. More than once I heard her whispering about Summerleigh and Daddy, but she didn't speak ill of either in front of me. Unfortunately, she wasn't the only one talking.

Everyone in town had talked when we left the West Desire Mobile Home Park for Summerleigh. People thought we were fools before, and they knew for sure we were now, Momma complained to Aunt Dot and me. But the thick-tongued gossips didn't deter Daddy. He didn't care when folks said that we were living above our means or that having Belles living at Summerleigh was like putting lipstick on a pig. We'd come from a long line of sharecroppers, and everyone in Desire knew it. But Daddy had brought us all up now, with his medals and many awards for bravery, so perhaps they would talk a bit less. That's what Aunt Dot told me even though her very own sister did not hold to that viewpoint.

I loved my Aunt Dot. People said I looked just like her, and when I was a child, I liked to fantasize that she—rather than the elegant but cold Ann Marie Belle—was my mother. If Momma had her choice, we'd all be back in the cramped trailer park where she could once again be the queen of her own social kingdom, of which Augustine Hogue was her chief ally.

Summerleigh had been a fine two-story mansion with five columns across the front porch and two smaller one-story wings on each side. Once upon a time, Summerleigh must have seemed a magical place, but by the time we carried our boxes and suitcases inside, it had stood empty for at least forty years. It felt less like a palace and more like a graveyard.

As with any small town, there was plenty of talk in Desire about the McIntyre family, the original owners of the house. Daddy quickly became obsessed with the McIntyre family history too. When he wasn't tinkering with something around the house, replacing wood here and there or scraping off old wallpaper, he was reading about them.

Yes, I remembered my first trip to Summerleigh. There had been a rickety gate and a broken walkway that led to the front door. The unkempt yard was full of untamed bushes and overgrown saw grass that hid things like field rats and a family of feral cats who dined on the rodents regularly. Oh, I hated finding those carcasses all over the place. One cat in particular liked to leave half-eaten rats on the front porch, as a kind of peace offering, I supposed.

Harper, are you coming?

Loxley's voice called to me now from somewhere beyond the noisy Dr. Odom's droning. Obviously, no one else heard her, and I was okay with that. I didn't want to share her. As he scribbled on his notepad, I announced, "I'm ready for a nap. Everyone out." Jerica frowned at me for my rudeness, but I was tired and Loxley was waiting.

They finally left me alone, and I breathed a sigh of relief. I had done what I needed to do; Jerica had promised to bring my sister home, to find Jeopardy Belle. I could rest now. Old age had finally caught up with the unstoppable Harper Belle Hayes, and I had done all I could do. I lay down on my bed and closed my eyes. Oh, I was so tired, much too tired to do one more thing.

But the peaches need washing and the quilts need beating, Harper. Momma needs you...

"Alright, Momma," I said to my memory. Now I remembered the poem. I recalled it perfectly!

Monday's child is fair of face
Tuesday's child is full of grace
Wednesday's child is full of woe,
Thursday's child has far to go
Friday's child is loving and giving
Saturday's child works hard for a living
But the child who is born on the Sabbath day
Is bonnie and blithe, and good and gay....

I could hear their voices, young girl voices all sing-song-y. Patent leather shoes tapped the floors as they jumped in time.

Harper...come on, slowpoke. Why do you have to be dead last at everything?

"Jeopardy?" I whispered. "Is that you?"

"Of course, dummy. Get your head out of the clouds and come on. How are we going to double-jump without you?"

I ran up the second set of stairs now. I could hear my sisters jumping rope in the big empty room on the top floor. That was the best place to jump rope when it rained. And it was raining now. I raced to the doorway, and my hands were on the doorframe. My eyes were closed, and I couldn't face it if I opened them and they were ghosts. I didn't want to see them like that.

Please don't be horrible, I thought. *Don't be ghosts!*

The rain stopped, and I felt comforting warmth, like the sun shining on my face. I opened my eyes and without a second thought walked into the room.

I was home at Summerleigh. Jeopardy smiled at me and handed me one of the ropes. I had found her after all! I kissed her cheek and took my place across from Addison. As always, Loxley and Jeopardy would jump first. I had questions for Jeopardy, so many questions, but strangely enough, I could remember none of them at the moment.

Monday's child...we began to sing together. Our shoes tapped, we sang, and I realized I was young again. My hands were young; I wore my pink dress, the one with the strawberries on the collar and hem.

I was home now, and I would never leave again.

Chapter Three—Jerica

I had been mistaken about Eddie's theft; he'd taken more than my fifty dollars. He stole my bank card too. How could I have missed that? Fortunately, my bank called my cell phone to notify me that there had been unusual activity on my card. I told them my wallet had been stolen, which was partly true. They were going to investigate, but as it stood now, my ex-husband had cleaned out both my checking and savings accounts. The bank encouraged me to file a police report, and luckily for me—or unluckily, however you wanted to look at it—I had a contact at the police department. I pulled Detective Michelle Easton's card out of my purse and called her the first chance I got.

During a long, embarrassing conversation, I explained what happened. She said, "I'll get the papers started, but you'll need to come by and sign them so I can start recouping your money. Over three grand, huh? Mr. Poole is looking at a felony or two with this one. And you still want to do this?"

"I don't have any choice this time, Detective. The bank insists on having a police report of the theft, and frankly, I don't know of any other way to get him the help he needs."

Easton went quiet as if she were thinking about my statement but didn't offer any advice. "I'll have it ready when you get here. Do you have somewhere to stay this evening?"

"Uh, no. Why?"

"Well, he may have a key to your apartment. You need to change the locks."

I glanced over my shoulder. Someone was coming into the break room, and I wouldn't be able to keep my shameful secret to myself with a dozen ears in here. It was bad enough that Anita knew. It was almost time to go anyway. "I don't have the money for that right now. He stole it! Besides, I don't have anything left for him to take. He's got my medication and my money."

"Wait, you didn't say he took your medication. That's another felony, possession of a controlled substance for starters. Whatever you do, come by here when you can. The sooner we get started, the better the chance we find him with at least some of your cash."

"Alright, I'm leaving now."

"Great, see you in my office."

I hung up, retrieved my purse and headed out with a wave to Marcheline, the evening supervisor. "See you later." Pausing in the doorway, I considered saying goodbye to Harper, but she'd been sleeping the last time I peeked in on her.

"Wait up, Jerica," Anita called to me.

"Yes?" I put a fake smile on my face.

"I'm not trying to be nosy, but you take this." She shoved a crumpled bill in my hand. "No argument. You do what you have to. If you need anything else, you let me know." She hugged me quickly and left me standing on the damp sidewalk. Opening my hand, I was surprised to find a hundred-dollar bill.

So that had been Anita in the break room. Well, I knew she would keep a confidence, and I was sure going to pay her back. I tucked the money into my pocket and climbed into my rust bucket. I leaned back in the seat pondering what I wanted to do. Two felonies? How long would that add up to? Obviously, Eddie would do prison time; he'd escaped that fate twice already, but this time...this time would be the real deal. And I would be the one to send him there. I believed what I had told the detective, that this would be the only way he would get any help, but now I was halting between two minds.

What should I do? Take the financial loss and let him slide or be the one to turn the key in the lock? Screw it. He didn't care about me or my pain. All he cared about was himself. I had to do this or else I would be letting him take me down with him.

I am sorry, Marisol. I am so sorry about your Daddy.

I heard nothing except my cell phone ringing. Unknown number...did I dare answer it? Of course, responsible me, I had to. What if it was a doctor or someone from my medical staff?

"Hello?"

"Hey, Jerica. Don't hang up."

"Don't hang up? Are you crazy calling me? I want my money back, Eddie, and my medication! You robbed me, you bastard. Me, of all people! You robbed me!" I didn't mean to start sobbing, but I did. It didn't last long.

"If you would let me explain...please, Jerica. Marisol..."

"Don't you dare mention her name! Don't you dare!"

"I lost a daughter too, Jerica."

Then I said the meanest thing I could think of, and saying it brought me no joy. "Well, at least she won't have to see what a complete failure you've become." Eddie went silent, but I knew he was still there. "The cops are looking for you, Eddie, and I am going to tell them every place I think you'll be. Every place! Don't you ever contact me again. Don't even say my name, or hers! You're dead to me!"

"You're an ice cold bitch, Jerica! Ice cold! You hear me? You turn me into the cops, and I'll make you regret it. Marisol is gone because of you! You killed my..."

I hung up on him and tossed the phone on the passenger side floorboard so I couldn't pick it up. I went straight to the police station and signed on every dotted line Detective Easton asked me to.

"What are your plans for tonight? Are you still staying at the apartment?" she asked me.

"No, I'm going to a hotel, but I have to get some clothes first."

Easton got up and slid on her jacket. "Alright, let's go. I'll drop this off at the Warrant Division, and then we'll go together. I don't trust him, Mrs. Poole. If he's got the cajones to rob you, of all people, there's no telling what else he'd do." I didn't tell her about his latest phone call. Why add years to the sentence? He was a low-down, dirty, backstabbing bastard, and I wanted her to find him. And I agreed with the detective. Eddie was perfectly capable of hurting me. I would have never believed it before all this, but now? Absolutely.

"Thank you."

An hour later, I was checking into a local hotel. I took the detective's advice and got a room that could only be accessed from the inside, and I parked my car away from the building. I missed my apartment and hoped that Easton would nab Eddie quickly so I could return home without fear of repercussions.

After eating a bland meal from the hotel grill and showering, I felt kind of human and decided to try and get some sleep. I had forgotten to pack socks, and my feet were freezing. I shoved them under the covers and eventually fell asleep. I don't know how long I slept, but it couldn't have been too long. Or at least it didn't feel like it. I pretended that I didn't hear the phone ringing on the nightstand. It couldn't be good news. I didn't pick it up.

As I drifted off to sleep, I heard a young woman's voice calling me. At first it sounded like she was underwater, but then her voice became clearer. I could see her now. Her bobbed hair was pinned back on the left, and she wore a pink dress with strawberries embroidered on the collar and hem. She was tall and pretty and oh so familiar.

"Harper?" I whispered. She stretched her hand out to me, and I took it. I wondered if I was dead but didn't voice the question. Instead, I followed her, and then she disappeared.

I was somewhere I had never been before, but I knew where I was. Somehow, I knew.

I was at Summerleigh.

Chapter Four—Harper

July 1942

Momma's shiny black Chevy Master DeLuxe raced up the driveway toward Summerleigh, leaving a wide trail of dust in its wake. It was hot and sticky out; we needed rain to tamp down the powdery red dirt, but no luck so far. Momma and Augustine Hogue had gone shopping this morning in Momma's new car, a gift from her father, Mr. Daughdrill. Although he was our grandfather, we weren't allowed to call him Grandpa or anything like that; he preferred Mr. Daughdrill. I had no idea what Momma had done to earn such a vehicle. Our grandfather rarely appeared in our lives, only when my father wasn't around. There was no love lost between the two, that much was certain, but Momma had always stood by Daddy in her own selfish way.

Momma and Miss Augustine were laughing as they walked through the back door. Momma deposited her shopping bags on the kitchen table and walked through to the parlor without even a hello to me. The ladies removed their hats and took their seats by the radio. Amanda of Honeymoon Hill would come on in a few minutes, and they never missed their favorite program. Sometimes my sister Addison joined them, but not today. She remained in her bed with a toothache; it was less a toothache and more a heartache. I reminded her that Daddy would be gone for only a few weeks this time; this deployment was much shorter than the others. Daddy had a very special mission to accomplish, I told her, but it hadn't helped. Daddy was a larger-than-life figure, a handsome man with a beaming smile and a deep devotion to his Belles. He had been our hero before the war, and now he had become a hero to our entire community. Nobody could put him down now. He'd saved too many men, rescued too many soldiers for those naysayers to continue their mockery of John Jeffrey Belle.

Jeopardy was sulking somewhere upstairs. As soon as Daddy left the house, she began writing him a long letter, probably berating him for leaving or some such nonsense. Jeopardy wrote him daily while he was gone, although she wasn't always allowed to mail her letters. Momma would fuss about the cost of postage and remind Jeopardy that Daddy had better things to do than write letters to a girl. He had work to do, but that didn't discourage Jeopardy. She'd find a way to earn change enough to mail her letters.

I wrote Daddy too, but not nearly as much as Jeopardy did. I had other responsibilities like cooking supper, cleaning the house and caring for the garden. Besides, Daddy didn't write me back, not like he did with Jeopardy. And in the end, I didn't want to compete with my sister for Daddy's affections. Addison never wrote him because writing gave her headaches, she said, and little Loxley could barely write her name. Heaven knows if Momma ever wrote him, but he certainly sent her cards, letters and gifts all the way from Europe. Jeopardy always ended up with those trinkets; otherwise, they might find their way to a pawn shop or a yard sale. Momma didn't treasure Daddy's gifts like we did.

The ladies were laughing about something. I already had the tea brewed and cooling on the counter. And then the intro music came on and they grew quiet. I poured two glasses of tea, broke off a few pieces of ice from inside the freezer, dropped them in the glasses and carried them to the parlor. Out of the corner of my eye, I saw Jeopardy skulking on the stairs, but I didn't give her position away; I didn't have to. Momma spied her and called her down during the opening commercial. Amanda of Honeymoon Hill always had lots of advertisements at the beginning of the broadcast. I think I liked those better than the actual program. Someday I would get to try that fancy new Pepti Toothpaste.

"What are you wearing, Jeopardy? Is that the same dress you wore yesterday?" Momma frowned at her oldest daughter as she walked toward her. "And when was the last time you brushed your hair...or your teeth? Come here and stop slouching." Jeopardy didn't obey her. She stood with her hips shifted to the left, her right hand grasping the upper part of her left arm. Clearly, she didn't want to be anywhere near our mother. She always blamed her for Daddy's deployment, and even I didn't appreciate Momma's joyous attitude in his absence.

Miss Augustine huffed beside Momma as she cast a disapproving eye on the eldest Belle child. I wanted to intervene, but it would do me no good. No good at all. When Momma and Jeopardy tied up, it was best to stay out from between them. That had been Daddy's advice. You could just sense they were on a collision course for a fight, and I was getting nervous for Jeopardy. But then Momma smiled, her pretty face undeterred by her daughter's disobedience.

In a sweet, cheery voice, she said to Jeopardy, "There are two baskets of peaches on the kitchen counter. One goes to Mrs. Hendrickson and the other to Dr. Leland. Collect a quarter for each basket, or twenty cents if they want to return the baskets. You can take Loxley's red wagon if you think you can't carry them both."

"All the way to Leland's? That's over a mile away," Jeopardy whined.

"And the sooner you get started, the sooner you'll get back, but please tidy up before you leave. I can't have you leaving the house looking like you stepped out of a pigpen, Jeopardy Belle."

Jeopardy was ready to argue about it, I could tell. This was my chance to defuse the situation and save my sister from further humiliation. "I'll go with you, Jeopardy. I'd like to return Mrs. Hendrickson's paperbacks anyway."

"No!" Momma said sharply before the smile returned to her face. "Miss Hogue and I will need your help with canning that bushel of peaches in the sink, Harper. Why don't you start peeling them while Jeopardy runs this errand for me? And of course, you'll keep ten cents for yourself, Jeopardy, dear. I'm sure you'll want to buy paper and postage stamps for all those letters."

Jeopardy's face lit up, and she scampered back up the steps to brush her hair and her teeth and maybe change her dress. I was disappointed that I couldn't go, but at least I would be in the kitchen near the open window and not traipsing around in this heat. Five minutes later, as the ladies were deeply immersed in their radio program, Jeopardy loaded two baskets onto Loxley's Radio Flyer and headed down the lane. She didn't say much except goodbye, and I could see from the kitchen window that she was taking the shortcut through the woods. *Good for her.* The trip wouldn't be quite a mile long, and she'd have plenty of shade. I noticed she carried her favorite stick, just in case she needed to knock a snake in the head. We had plenty of black snakes around here. Summerleigh wasn't that far from Dog River, and the snakes got stirred up even more on hot days like this one.

After the radio program, Momma and Miss Augustine came into the kitchen. I assumed they were going to help me peel the peaches, but Momma had her hat on. "I'm taking Miss Augustine home. She has an appointment she forgot all about, but I will be back in a few minutes to help you." As soon as she opened the screen door, she paused. "It looks like it might storm soon. Have Loxley come inside, Harper. We don't want her to get sick, and you know she's prone to keep a runny nose in the summer."

"Alright, Momma. Could you check on Jeopardy? She might get caught in the rain, and I see lightning just up the road."

Her face tightened, and her eyes flashed at me. "I am sure she's on her way home now, Harper. Don't worry about Jeopardy; she's a resourceful young lady."

"I don't know how resourceful she'll be in a rainstorm," I whispered to her back as she stepped off the porch with Miss Augustine's bulky frame in tow. I washed my hands in the sink and went looking for Loxley. I hadn't seen her all morning, and finding her would be a chore. I didn't need another chore; I had a sneaking suspicion that I would be canning this bushel of peaches by myself.

"Loxley, come in the house. It's going to rain!" I yelled at the edge of the yard. I didn't have time to go wandering through the woods. "Loxley! You hear me? Come back to the house!" I waited around and didn't hear a thing. With a sigh of exasperation, I walked to the front of the house just in case. Loxley generally didn't venture into the unkempt front yard; she had a great fear of rodents, and there were usually plenty scrabbling around out here. But she did have a tendency to wander...especially when accompanied by one of her invisible friends.

"Loxley!" I didn't see hide nor hair of her, but after listening for a moment I heard her voice coming from the house. Sing-songy, like she was playing a hand-clapping or jump rope game with someone, but who? Jeopardy was gone, Addison was down in the bed, and here I was. You sure couldn't play a hand-clapping game with a ghost, could you? I would have to go fetch her and bring her downstairs before Momma got back home. Momma didn't like us to "lurk around up there," as she described it. Some of the floors were spongy and might give way if you trod on them, she warned us repeatedly.

I went around to the back door and through to the kitchen and peeked in on Addison. No, she was still there, sleeping in her bed. I walked back through the Great Room to the parlor and then up the first set of stairs. Suddenly, I heard footsteps running away from me.

"Loxley? Please don't make me chase you."

I waited, but she never came down the stairs. With an exasperated sigh, I climbed the steps. The footsteps returned, only this time they weren't running away from me but coming up behind me. "Jeopardy?" I turned, expecting to see her returned from her errand, but there was no one there. My skin suddenly felt icy cold as if I had stepped into an icehouse. My stomach did a double-clutch, but I didn't wait to ponder it. I scampered up the stairs away from the mysterious sounds in search of Loxley.

"Loxley Belle, you come out here right now."

"Up here..." she called from the floor above.

As quietly as I could, I raced to the end of the hall and ran up the stairs uncaring if they were spongy or not. The invisible footsteps had put the fear of God in me, and I didn't want to be up here. I couldn't shake the feeling that someone was behind me, following me, watching me.

"Loxley!"

"Here, silly. In the nursery." And there she was, sitting on the floor by the window, a sprinkling of jacks and a tiny red rubber ball in front of her. "Play with me, Harper."

I could see the dark clouds gathering through the dirty, curtainless window. I didn't care for this room. It had too many nooks and crannies, too many places for things to hide. "Loxley, who was in here? I heard footsteps on the stairs, and I heard you clapping hands with someone. Someone was up here. Who was it?"

"That boy. I think you scared him away. He doesn't like grown-ups."

"I'm no grown-up," I said with a nervous, uncertain smile. "What boy? Someone I know?" I sat down across from her. She picked up the ball and stared at me with her big blue eyes.

"No, I don't think so. He ran out of the room when he heard you coming. Will you play with me?"

A shadow passed by the door, but I pretended I didn't see it. Loxley glanced behind her and then turned back to me with curious eyes. I said, "I can play for just a minute or two. I have to finish peeling peaches before Momma gets back. I'm waiting on Jeopardy too. She went to deliver jars, and it's going to storm."

"Play with me first and I will help you, Harper," she promised with her sweetest expression.

"You mean you'll eat them all. Come on, then, you first."

We played a few rounds, and then I reminded her of my chore. Tucking the jacks and ball in her pin-striped apron pocket, she paused and stared at the doorway. I couldn't discern her expression. "What is it, Loxley?"

"I think we should go now."

The hair on my arms prickled up as I asked, "Why? Is someone coming?" I didn't hear any footsteps, but ghosts didn't always let you know they were there until they jumped out at you. At least that's what Loxley told me.

She nodded and took my hand. "We have to go, and Momma will be back soon." We were down two flights of stairs in no time flat. I didn't ask any more questions and gladly went back to paring peaches. Just as Loxley predicted, Momma returned without Miss Augustine and chattered away as she got the pot ready for the jars. The three of us worked together to get the peaches on to simmer, and Momma even allowed Loxley to add a dash or two extra of cinnamon. Loxley loved cinnamon.

Without my hearing her arrive, Jeopardy stormed in through the back door looking like she'd fallen down a hill. The sleeve of her dress was torn, her face was dirty, and there could be no doubt she'd been crying.

Momma didn't say a word, but I couldn't help but exclaim, "Jeopardy!" My sister didn't speak but stared at Momma with all the hatred she could muster. To my surprise, Momma smiled sweetly. What was happening? Suddenly, Jeopardy threw the quarters and a handful of twenty-dollar bills at Momma, but Momma didn't flinch. Jeopardy ran through the kitchen away from us all. Our mother continued to stir the pot and didn't go see about her. I went instead.

It was her footsteps I heard now. I knew the sound of her shoes well. She bounded up the stairs two by two all the way to her "castle" room in the attic. I heard her lock it, but I refused to go away.

"Jeopardy, it's me, Harper. Please let me in." The only sound I heard was her crying. "Please, Jeopardy."

She didn't answer me. After a few minutes, I walked down the hallway and waited at the top of the stairs. What could I do? I couldn't force her to open the door. A hundred horrible scenarios played in my head, but I couldn't figure out what just happened. Maybe Momma knew. I would certainly ask her. I looked back once more and to my surprise saw a woman in a white gown with long dark hair sliding through the locked door. And then Jeopardy's crying stopped.

I didn't stay at Summerleigh. I had never seen a ghost before, and the experience left me terrified. Ignoring Momma's call, I ran until I couldn't run anymore and found myself clear down the lane at Mrs. Hendrickson's yard. As always, the older woman was home, and I went inside and cried on her shoulder. I couldn't explain why I was so upset, but after a few hours, a half-dozen tea cakes and a phone call from Momma, I was prepared to go back to Summerleigh.

Or as prepared as I could be.

Chapter Five—Jerica

Taking an extra five minutes in the shower, I stood under the showerhead dumbfounded at the memory of my strange dream. In no way did I think I had imagined any of it. There was no doubt in my mind that Harper Belle Hayes had visited me and that I'd seen life through her eyes for a little while. As I scrubbed my body, I could smell traces of Harper's lavender perfume, taste the peaches on my lips and feel the heat of that long-ago summer day on my skin. Yes, I had been there. Loxley's curious eyes and Jeopardy's ripped sleeve came back to my mind; these were images I would never forget—not in a lifetime. I wasn't sure how Harper had done it, but she and I had connected in that dream, and I couldn't wait to talk to her about it. I knew for a fact my friend was a big believer in dreams, since she shared hers with me often, but this was certainly an unusual experience. I used to dream all the time, but I never did anymore since Marisol's death. Until now.

I rinsed the soap off my skin and stepped out of the hotel's shower surprised to hear my cell phone ringing. "Shoot," I complained to no one. I wrapped a towel around my body and another around my hair before padding off to the nightstand to retrieve my phone. Someone from the front desk of the care facility had called. Some emergency must have happened. I glanced at the bright red alarm clock display. I would be at work in thirty minutes, just as I was supposed to be, but I couldn't avoid returning the call. I was the administrator, and I couldn't shirk my responsibilities despite my current personal drama. There could only be a few reasons why anyone from work would call so close to check-in time. And none of them were good.

To my surprise, it wasn't Marcheline who answered the phone but Anita. "Good morning, this is Jerica."

Anita answered, "I am sorry to call you like this when I know you'll be here soon, but I have to give you this notice. Can't avoid procedure even though..."

"Notice? Who passed away, Anita?" I asked as I sat on the bed. I knew exactly who died, but my mind wasn't willing to process the heartbreaking truth.

"It's Miss Harper. She's gone, Jerica. Passed away in her sleep. I am so sorry."

My hands shook at the news. "Um, I'll be there soon, Anita. Thank you."

"Take your time. We're just getting her ready now, but the ambulance is here for her. Do you want them to wait for you?"

"No, that's not necessary. You sign the paperwork, okay?" This was one patient I couldn't say goodbye to. Not like that.

"You've got it. I'll see you soon."

Anita hung up, and I collapsed on the bed. This explained everything, how Harper came to me in my dream, how she could share a bit of her life with me.

She was dead.

Then I remembered the picture I had placed on my nightstand last night. I stared at those hopeful faces now. There they were: Jeopardy, Harper, Addison and Loxley. All of the Belle girls except for Jeopardy were smiling back at me.

I tucked the picture and my phone back in my leather purse, finished getting dressed and checked out of the hotel. *Screw Eddie. I'm not staying away from home another night.* I needed to go to my apartment anyway—I needed to brush my teeth and change into clean underwear. I had been so frazzled that I'd forgotten to pack underwear and my toothbrush as well as socks. I couldn't face the day with fuzzy teeth, and I wasn't one to go "commando" as my old roommate used to. That would put me getting to work even later. Well, it couldn't be avoided. With my hair still wet and with minimal makeup, I made the drive to my apartment and raced up the stairs to find that my door stood open.

Oh, God. Not this.

Without thinking, I stepped inside and immediately noticed that my television and satellite receiver were missing. The couch cushions were scattered as if someone had taken the time to dig for change—or knew exactly where I kept my "mad money" in a zippered plastic bag. I should have known it would be a bad idea to hide money in the couch.

"Hello?" I called, but nobody answered. As cold as it was in here, the door must have been open for hours. *Gee, I have great neighbors. Did nobody hear all this commotion?* The kitchen didn't have much missing except the microwave, but my bedroom looked a shambles. Someone had pulled out all the dresser drawers, and my clothes were all over the floor. My nightstands and closet stood open, and my computer and jewelry boxes were gone. I sat on the bare mattress and took in the sight.

Oh no! Eddie had taken Marisol's picture! The one from our last day at the beach. I checked around to see if it had fallen on the floor, but there wasn't a trace. He'd clearly stolen it as if in one last cruel act, he would steal her memory from me. Eddie wasn't joking. He clearly blamed me for the accident; he blamed me that Marisol was gone.

God, I had been such a fool to let him back in here. What the hell, Eddie?!

When I quit sobbing, I knew I had to call the police. Again. I'd left my cell phone in my purse, so I had to use the landline. Picking up the phone, I heard a voice on the line. A girl's voice. Nothing but whispers, desperate whispers. "Hello?" I said as I sprang to my feet. There was another phone in the living room. What if someone was hurt? I ran through the mess and raced to the phone. It was still on its receiver. There was no one in here. I hung up the phone and picked it up again and again, but nothing I did disconnected the sad voice. Whoever was there didn't hang up, and she was crying now. The whispers continued, and the voice sounded even more heartbreaking.

"Hello? Is someone there?"

"What happened in here?" Detective Easton stood in the doorway. I dropped the phone and nearly jumped a foot off the ground.

"You tell me. I thought you guys were watching this place! If I had to guess, I'd say that Eddie cleaned me out while I was hiding out in the hotel. What a great idea to leave my home unattended!" Angry words burst out of my mouth before I had a chance to think about reining myself in. Harper's death and now this? It was too much to handle.

"He's a likely candidate, but we can't know for sure he did this until we begin the investigation. Could you have left it unlocked?"

I ignored her stupid question, tossed a couch cushion on the couch and sat on it. "Well, he took my change stash, and nobody knew about that bag of change except Eddie. It was right here."

"Lots of people hide money in their couch, Jerica."

I shook my head and said, "You honestly think a stranger did this?"

"Could be a stranger, but Eddie Poole would be my first suspect. First things first, I'll need you to step out; this is a crime scene now. I have to get the crime team in here, and I'll need a list of what's missing."

"Marisol's picture, the one on my nightstand—he took it. It had to be him. Who else would do such a thing?"

"I am sorry, Jerica. We let you down on this one, but I'll get to the bottom of this."

I didn't believe her. I knew it wasn't going to be all right. I was never going to be rid of Eddie. He would always torment me, blame me for Marisol's death. Like I didn't blame myself enough. "I don't have time for this. I have to go to work—a patient has passed away. You do what you have to, Detective."

"Oh, sorry to hear that. Alright. Well, I'll call you when we're done."

"Fine," I said. "And don't bother locking the door. There's nothing left to steal."

I was too stunned to cry now. I drove to work feeling numb, just like the morning of the accident. One minute we'd been singing, and the next....

The ambulance was parked in front of the doors, and I watched as the paramedics respectfully wheeled the sheet-covered body of Harper Hayes out of the Sunrise Retirement Home. Some of the residents came to watch her leave; this would be hard on them. Harper had been everyone's favorite. Even the crotchety Ricky Jackson liked her, and that was saying a lot.

When the ambulance drove off, I wiped away tears and walked inside. This would be the second hardest day of my life.

Chapter Six—Jerica

Anita and I had barely finished Harper's paperwork when an older gentleman in a tidy blue suit appeared at my station. "May I help you, sir?"

"I'm here on business for Mrs. Harper Hayes."

Anita and I looked at one another. "I'm sorry to tell you that Mrs. Hayes passed away this morning. Were you a family member?" I asked politely.

"Yes, I know about her passing, but I am not a family member. I am a friend of hers from Mississippi."

Curious about who this unknown friend could be, I suggested that we speak privately in one of the empty consultation rooms. Closing the door behind us, I invited Harper's visitor to sit across from me at the small, round table. It was then that I noticed the man had a small leather bag with him. He put it on the table and unzipped it with trembling hands.

"I didn't catch your name, sir. I am Jerica Poole."

"Oh, good, just the lady I wanted to see." He removed two envelopes, one small and the other long and white. He placed the smaller one in front of me. "I am supposed to give you this, in the event of Harper's passing." He slid the sealed envelope closer to me. I didn't open it.

"What's this all about?" The hair pricked up on the back of my neck, but I kept an uneasy smile on my face.

"I know this all appears so mysterious, but I am here on behalf of Harper Belle. Excuse me, Harper Belle Hayes. My name is Ben, Ben Hartley. I am an old friend of the Belle family, specifically Harper. I haven't seen much of Harper in the past few years, but that wasn't entirely my fault."

Shaking my head, I said, "Not to doubt you, but she never mentioned having a friend named Ben. Again, I'm not trying to be rude..."

He sighed sadly. "I can believe it. I think she spent most of her life trying to forget me, but I never forgot her. I would have thought she had forgiven me after all this time. She must have, or she wouldn't have sent me here. Please take the envelope. It is meant for you."

I licked my suddenly dry lips and said, "I can't accept the envelope, Ben. First, I don't know what's in it, and second, as an employee of the Sunrise Retirement Home, it's against the rules to accept gifts from residents, past or present. As you say, you're here on Harper's behalf. So this would be considered a gift from her, or whatever this is. I am sure you understand; I have to follow the rules." That wasn't entirely true, considering the gifts Harper had given me for Marisol, but I didn't want to offend him.

Ben's wrinkled face reddened, and his faded green eyes were moist with unshed tears. He had a head full of hair, but I could tell he wasn't in the best of health. In this line of work, I had learned to pick up on these things pretty quickly. "Harper said you would be the one to help her find Jeopardy. It was her last wish, Miss Poole."

I didn't correct him on calling me Miss, but my face reddened too. "I have every intention of doing my research, Mr. Hartley, but I can't accept money."

"It's not money. It's the keys to Summerleigh and the caretaker's cottage. I used to live there. The cottage is still in working order. If you'd like, I can have it cleaned and updated before you arrive."

"I think there's been some mistake, sir." A nervous laugh escaped my lips. "I am not going to Summerleigh. Harper never asked me to move to Mississippi."

"How else will you find Jeopardy? You can't do that from a desk in Virginia. No, hear me out. All of the Belles are gone now, even little Loxley. There is no one left, no one to carry on the search." His shoulders sagged, and although I felt horrible for bringing him any discomfort, I had to be honest with him. I was nothing if not honest.

"What about the sheriff's department or a detective agency? I've never looked for a missing person before. Harper was my friend, Ben. She helped me through the most difficult time in my life. I am not exaggerating when I tell you that I loved Harper like a mother. I think it's a great tragedy, the disappearance of her sister, but I don't know why she believes I can help bring her home. I'm not a family member."

"Sometimes blood isn't thicker than water, Miss Poole. It's about the ties of the heart, not your genetic makeup. And I am sorry for your loss."

Not half as sorry as I am, I thought. I peeked inside the envelope. Sure enough, there were two brass keys inside and a slip of paper with an address written on it.

"Would you mind if I visited the restroom?" he asked politely. The phone rang in and surprised the heck out of me. Only Anita knew I was in here, so I knew it must be important. I picked it up hurriedly and covered the receiver.

"Of course, Ben. It's just around the corner to the right."

"Thank you." His southern drawl was very apparent now. Funny how I didn't notice it at the beginning of our conversation. It was almost as if the more tired he appeared, the thicker his accent.

"Yes, Anita?"

"I have the funeral home on the line. They have some questions for you—they say they can't wait. Can you take their call now?"

"No, let me wrap this up and I'll call them back. I mean, surely they can wait five minutes."

"Alright," she said and hung up.

I rolled the chair back to the table and picked up the envelope again. How long had Harper been planning this, and how in the world did her old friend Ben Hartley know she'd passed away so quickly? No way he made the drive up from Mississippi in just a few hours. I tapped on the desk as I waited for the return of the mysterious Mr. Hartley. How exactly did he know Harper? It sounded like something serious had passed between them. How could I politely ask such a question? *Curiosity killed the cat.* After a couple of minutes, I walked out to the office and waited in the hall. Anita raised her dark eyebrows at me.

"Where did he go?"

"The old man?"

"Yes, Ben Hartley."

"He left five minutes ago."

"What? He left his stuff in here." I walked back in the office and was surprised to see that his leather bag was gone but not the two envelopes. With shaking fingers, I opened the larger envelope. I couldn't believe my eyes. This was Harper's Last Will and Testament.

I read the document aloud just to make sure I wasn't losing my mind.

I, Harper Belle Hayes, hereby bequeath all my worldly possessions, including my home, Summerleigh, to my dear friend, Jerica Jernigan Poole...

Chapter Seven—Jerica

I parked the SUV in the driveway and sat for a minute; how amazing was it that I'd actually made it in one piece? I'd never been an adventurous person, and except for my senior trip, this was the first time I'd left the state of Virginia. And I'd certainly never been the one to do the driving; Eddie always commandeered the wheel for any day trips we went on. But look at me now. Here I was! I got out of the vehicle to stretch my legs. Driving for two days had left me feeling stiff all over. I slammed the car door and dug my hands into my back pockets as I stretched my back.

Summerleigh had undergone recent repairs. Even from just halfway up the length of the driveway, I smelled fresh cut lumber and sawdust. And I knew sawdust. My foster parents had owned a lumberyard, and I had spent many a happy day playing with blocks and piles of dust. The historic home had five columns that lined the front porch. Yes, there were two one-story wings flanking either side of the two-story main house, exactly as Harper had described it. The wing to the left needed some roof repair, and a massive tree branch lay next to it. *That must have been the culprit. They say this area of the south has incredible summer storms. Someone will have to trim some of these trees back because a few of those limbs look a bit dangerous.*

Besides the roof damage to the west wing, Summerleigh needed major siding repairs and a fresh coat of paint from top to bottom. That was just what I could see from the exterior. I noticed a wisteria vine loaded with purple blooms wrapping around the porch railing. Fat bumblebees were taking an interest in it too, and although the purple flowers gave the place a "lost in time" vibe, the vine would have to go. Or at least be cut back from the wooden railing.

Dad's words came back to me: *"You have to protect the wood, Jeri."*

See, Dad, I listened sometimes. You would love this place. I wish you could be here to see it. I protected my eyes from the glare of the sun with my hand as I stared at the top-floor windows. No glass had been broken, even though no one had called the place home in nearly thirty years. Still, the punch list was growing. The roof repairs, then a paint job, and who knew what I would find inside. The front lawn had been cared for, thankfully. Back when Harper first arrived here, the front yard looked like a jungle. Someone had obviously taken pride in keeping up with the gardening. Dark-leafed camellia bushes bloomed in neat flower beds in front of the house, and the white blooms gave the place an inviting look, like a postcard. The front porch light fixture had been replaced recently too. A grand black pendant light hung over the white porch below. Was I really doing this?

Well, Harper. I'm here. Now what?

I climbed back in the vehicle and drove to the back of Summerleigh. The back of the house was not as impressive as the front. A forlorn-looking circular courtyard was behind the house, and several gravel pathways disappeared into unkempt gardens. I followed the driveway around the courtyard and down a short drive that led to the caretaker's cottage. If you could call it that. The cottage was a smaller replica of Summerleigh, without the wings. Now this place was beautiful! It was a two-story home with painted whiteboards and two columns, one on each end of the front porch.

Anita, you're never going to believe this.

I immediately sent my friend a text and snapped a picture to go along with it. Like me, she could hardly believe Harper's generosity, but she'd supported me every step of the way since my decision to leave Sunrise. After the mysterious Ben Hartley's visit, everything in my life fell apart. Or maybe it fell into place.

Nightmares of the accident returned, and Eddie vandalized my vehicle several times. The detective couldn't locate him, but no matter where I hid out, Eddie always found me. And that was heartbreaking because I really wanted to help him—even after all the heartache. Losing Marisol had just about destroyed us both, but I'd managed to pull myself back up, thanks to my work. Eddie couldn't do that, and for whatever reason, the drugs, the grief, whatever...he blamed me for all of it. As if I were responsible for what happened to my baby, my only child. Guilt rose unbidden within me, but I immediately forced my mind to focus on what was in front of me. No, I wouldn't travel down memory lane today. This was my life now. The only regret I had was leaving my daughter behind.

Naturally, I had to give up my job. My employers weren't happy about the inheritance, and I certainly couldn't tell them that Harper wanted me to find her sister. But again, thanks to Harper, I had several thousand dollars in the bank with more to come later and a house that needed my attention. Not to mention a mystery that needed solving. Would I really be able to find Jeopardy Belle? What if I couldn't? If that was the case, I wouldn't stay. I couldn't do that in good conscience. I thought perhaps some heir would appear to claim the family home, maybe one of Addison's or Loxley's children. But nobody did. No one wanted Summerleigh. Nobody cared that Jeopardy had never been found.

So here I was in southern Mississippi, far away from home, and I felt invigorated. I hadn't expected to feel this level of "rightness," and it was a pleasant surprise. This had been the right thing to do. A raindrop hit my face and shook me out of my daydreaming. I grabbed my purse and hurried to the front door. I had a car to unpack, but it could wait. I slid the brass key in the door of the cottage and stepped inside. I was immediately met by a blast of cold air. Thank goodness the air conditioner worked in here. It was a bit too cold, though, I thought with a shiver.

"Wow," I said as I walked further into the inviting front room. The place had lovely hardwood floors, and there was a quilted rug in front of the wicker sofa. A beautiful window along the side of the room made the perfect picture frame for the greenery beyond. The sun was still partly shining, and rain had begun to fall softly. I spied a small patio and a bar-becue grill too. On the other side of the room were built-in oak bookcases, and I immediately went to check them out. I was impressed by how well made they were.

A small dining room was on the other side, with a kitchen just beyond that. The kitchen was small, but everything looked perfect. A vintage gas stove was against the far wall, and it looked neat and tidy. I loved the metal cabinets. Someone certainly had done a masterful job of keeping the place vintage but up to date. I opened the fridge; it was so clean it almost sparkled. I'd have to go to town today to stock the pantry. I doubted that anyone delivered out here. *What's upstairs?* Probably the bedroom and a full bath. A half bath was across the hall from the kitchen. As I set foot on the stairs to scamper up and check it out, I heard a polite knock on my door.

I opened it without worry. Eddie would never find me down here. Nobody knew where I was, except Anita, and she'd die before she told him anything.

"Hi, may I help you?" A striking man stood on my doorstep. He wore a handyman's clothes, and his welcoming smile was brilliant and warm.

"I was wondering the same thing. I was working in the potting shed and thought I heard someone pull in. You must be the new lady. Do you need any help?"

"Jerica Poole," I said as I extended my hand to him. "And so far, so good."

He didn't shake back, showing me his dirty palms. "You probably don't want to shake hands with me. My friends call me JB."

"Hi, JB. You been here long?"

"Yes, it's been awhile. You plan on sticking around? I was sad to see Ben go. It will be nice to have someone here to watch over the place."

"It's my privilege. I can't believe how beautiful this place is, and I haven't even been in the main house yet." I smiled, wondering if I should invite him in for a glass of... *Wait, I have no groceries.* "I'd invite you in for a glass of tea, but I haven't made it into town yet. Where's the best place to shop?"

"Up the road. Lucedale has a Piggly Wiggly. They'll have everything you need."

"Great. Well, JB, I'm sure I won't be as handy as Ben, but I'll try. Will I be able to find you if I need to ask you a question? Is there a phone number where I can reach you, or do you have a schedule or something?"

"No, I don't stay in one place long enough for a phone—or a schedule—but I am usually wandering around here. If you need anything, you'll probably find me in the potting shed. Just up the path there, toward the pond."

"There's a pond?" I asked incredulously.

"More like a mud hole, but we call it a pond," he joked with me.

"Great. I'll see you around, then."

He paused at the bottom of the steps and smiled once more before he walked away, a pot of dirt tucked under a muscular arm. He glanced back at me one more time, and I waved politely. The rain had stopped; even though I was on the front porch, I felt so cold that my teeth were nearly chattering. *God, I hope I'm not coming down with something.* Rubbing my arms to warm myself up, I decided this was the time to get my boxes moved. Hmm... why hadn't I asked JB to help me? Dummy. Oh well, I could handle it. I'd packed it all, taped it and loaded it up. I could certainly unload my own car.

It was dark before I finished, and I was too tired to investigate Summerleigh. Unlike the cottage, which was bright and cozy, the main house was completely dark. Not a light shone from any of the dusty windows. Was the power off? Well, I'd have to worry about that tomorrow.

I stowed the last of my stuff inside, unpacked a few boxes and decided I couldn't ignore my stomach any longer. Driving into town seemed like such a chore now. Strolling into my clean kitchen, I opened a few cabinets and found them stocked with basic grocery supplies.

Ben must have done this! In fact, I noticed he'd posted his phone number on the refrigerator with a Campbell's Soup magnet. I reached for a can of soup, quickly found a can opener and warmed the contents on the stove. Chicken noodle soup and a glass of water would be my supper, and that was all I needed. I cuddled up on the couch with a small quilt I found, white and pink with roses all over it. I loved it. With my stomach full and my back slightly sore, I drifted off to sleep.

And then Harper was there.

Chapter Eight—Harper

Even though Jeopardy and I were the oldest, Addison rode in the front seat of the Master DeLuxe this Sunday morning. Addie had a tendency to get sick if she rode in the back seat for any length of time. I didn't care much about who sat in the front seat, but Jeopardy did, and I could see her point of view. Jeopardy was a young lady now, the oldest of the Belle sisters, all of fifteen. And who wanted their friends to see them riding in the back seat? *It's the baby seat*, she complained quite loudly as we loaded up. It didn't matter to her that she didn't want to go to church to begin with. But she was here now, and I squeezed her hand once to reassure her before she snatched it away. I didn't know why she was so mad at me, but I was determined to make her smile again.

Come to think of it, making Jeopardy smile had been my lifelong ambition, at least when Daddy was away. Just think, in another week, he'd be home again. I had begun to count the days off on my dime store calendar, the one with the puppies on it. Of course, I didn't show it to anyone. The subject of Daddy's arrival seemed off-limits right now, and I couldn't understand why.

Momma was behind the wheel, complaining the entire time and honking her horn every few minutes. Loxley slept between us in the back seat, despite the noise. Here we were, in our Sunday best. Even Jeopardy wore a dress this morning, but I noticed she'd forgotten to wear a slip, which to our mother's mind wasn't ladylike at all. I hoped Momma didn't notice that oversight. We pulled into the driveway and waited for the dust to settle before we got out. Momma checked her teeth in the mirror and shot Jeopardy a disapproving look before she opened the door and stepped out.

Just as she did seven days a week, Momma looked like a movie star with her short blond hair and pretty features. Despite having four children, she had a trim waist and a perfect figure. "Come on, girls. Church is about to begin. Now remember, no sleeping or looking around like a wide-eyed calf. Are you listening, Loxley?"

"Yes, ma'am." Our sleepy sister took Momma's hand, and the rest of us walked behind her. I always loved coming to church, mostly because of the music. Sometimes the pastor told funny stories, and I liked those too. I got lost in the "thees" and "thous," but even that was entertaining.

Most Sundays, Jeopardy frowned the whole time, doodled on paper when she could and always, always did a lot of people-watching. Daddy never said anything to her, but things were different now—Daddy wasn't here. Unfortunately for Jeopardy, Momma settled herself between her and Loxley and didn't mind pinching Jeopardy's arm if she let herself get distracted. Momma didn't pinch me often, but it could hurt worse than a fire ant. And that was pretty bad. I fell in a fire ant bed once; I had bumps for weeks and would never forget the pain. Never.

We'd gotten through "Bringing in the Sheaves" with no incidents, except Jeopardy wouldn't sing and didn't care that Momma was cutting her eyes. She cracked gum instead, and I thought for sure she'd get backhanded for that. Sister Sheryl Sellers—she liked being called "sister," as did most of the church ladies—half-turned in her pew to see who the gum-cracking culprit was but didn't say a word. She did give Momma an offended look, though. As soon as the heavyset woman's head was turned, Momma held out her hand and waited for Jeopardy to spit out her gum. With a petulant expression, she dropped her gum in the waiting tissue.

The choir began singing again. *Do Lord, oh do Lord, oh, do remember me...* Loxley and I sang loudly, and Addison's soft voice obediently sang too. Jeopardy alone refused to praise the Lord even though Momma offered to share her red-backed hymnal with her. *Please, Jeopardy, behave yourself.* I kept my eyes in front of me, but I sensed impending disaster. So did Addison; she clutched her stomach, but I couldn't comfort her right now. I kept singing but silently prayed to the Good Lord for help.

Where is Aunt Dot this morning? She never misses Sunday Service. Please God, send Aunt Dot to church this morning. Help Jeopardy, God. Please save her, Jesus.

I called on the Father, Son and Holy Ghost, but the tension rose on our uncomfortable wooden pew— and we were surrounded by a church full of witnesses. Pastor Reed had just begun his sermon on the

Garden of Gethsemane when Jeopardy let out a yelp that shocked the entire congregation.

"Sit down!" Momma whispered like a freight train, but my sister wasn't having any of it. She was on her feet, her face like a dark cloud.

"Jeopardy," I whispered as she climbed over me with tears in her eyes. Momma hadn't gotten up yet, but she would in a moment if Jep didn't come back. She didn't.

Soon, all of us Belles were streaming out of the church and Momma and Jeopardy were having a shouting match in the parking lot. I didn't understand half of what they were saying, but my sister was yelling, her face red, and her bare, bruised arms gave evidence of Momma's cruel pinches. I didn't look back at the church, but I had a feeling that all fifty of the congregants were watching us from the arched windows of the First Baptist Church of Desire, Mississippi.

Loxley cried as Momma threatened to beat Jeopardy; Addison held her hand over her mouth as if she were going to throw up. Then like an angel from heaven, Aunt Dot pulled into the parking lot and scampered toward us. Her perfect bob bounced as she ran in heels toward Jeopardy, who was a screaming, crying mess.

"What in the world?" Aunt Dot asked as she gathered Jeopardy into her arms. "Ann, have you lost your mind arguing in the church parking lot? Oh great, here comes Augustine." Aunt Dot yelled to her, "Thank you, Augustine, but we're all fine here."

"She's incorrigible," Momma cried behind her handkerchief. "She'll ruin us all, Dorothy! Even Father says..."

"Ann, please. Don't say something you will regret later. I'll take Jeopardy home."

"She'll ride home with me, Dot. She's my daughter!"

Jeopardy sobbed on our aunt's shoulder. "No, dear," Aunt Dot answered calmly, "I think you need a break. You must be under so much stress with John Jeffrey gone. I will take Jeopardy home now. Have a cigarette or take the girls out for a soda. We will see you at Summerleigh." Aunt Dot didn't wait for an answer; she left with her arm around Jeopardy's shoulders.

Momma was silent as the grave on the drive home. We didn't stop for a soda, even though Addison whined about it until Momma popped her bare leg. I was suddenly glad that I wasn't in the front seat this morning. I blinked back the tears so Momma wouldn't see me cry. I couldn't be seen as taking sides, not if I wanted to smooth things over. If that was even possible now.

To my surprise, Aunt Dot's car was in the driveway when we got there. My sisters and I raced through the kitchen to avoid the coming battle. The Daughdrills rarely argued, but when they did, it was usually an epic event, although they never laid a hand on each other. I lingered outside the door for some morbid reason. Aunt Dot accused Momma of being cruel to Jeopardy; Momma called Aunt Dot a nosy spinster. I couldn't take any more of the accusations. I decided to tend to my sisters. They would need me, I believed. But Loxley didn't want a hug and instead went out the front door to go find one of her kittens. Addison headed to bed for a lie-down.

The only Belle missing was Jeopardy. She wasn't downstairs, so I knew she had to be in her castle room. I hated walking up the stairs, but today I would have risked walking through the gates of hell to help my sister. Why did it have to be this way? I vowed right then and there to write Daddy a letter. He had to know that his daughters needed him. Surely the Army would let him come home. I'd heard of soldiers coming home for emergencies before.

Jeopardy met me in the hallway. She'd shed her sundress and was wearing a pair of capris and a tank top; these were obviously some of Aunt Dot's hand-me-downs. Momma rarely bought Jeopardy an outfit, and Jeopardy hated the things Momma bought her and was quite vocal about that. Yes, she looked quite scandalous for a Sunday. Her hair hung loosely now, and over her shoulder was her crocheted purse. I pretended I didn't see a pack of Momma's cigarettes peeking out between the stitches. "Where are you going?" I asked in surprise.

"I'm going to the river. I'm meeting some friends there. If you care anything about me, you won't rat me out."

"I would never, Jeopardy. I never have!" I was offended at being accused of disloyalty. She should know that hurt me down to the bone.

She tilted her head and said, "Then come with me, Harper. Just for the day."

"What if Momma comes looking for me?"

"What if she does? Are you my sister or not?"

"Okay," I agreed without thinking it through any further. Jeopardy had challenged my loyalty, and I had to prove it to her. "I need to change, though."

"I'll meet you behind the potting shed. But I'm only waiting five minutes. If you don't come, if you chicken out, Harper, I'm gone."

"Alright. I'll be there."

Jeopardy and I tiptoed down the stairs, and she left out the back door to avoid another battle with Momma. Momma and Aunt Dot were still going at it, so I took advantage of the distraction and went to my bedroom and quickly changed into a checkered shirt and blue jean shorts. Grabbing my tennis shoes, I left Summerleigh, happy to leave the heated argument behind me. Loxley had her favorite kitten in her lap. She wouldn't miss me.

I ran around the house, avoiding the kitchen window, and found Jeopardy waiting for me by the shed. My rebellious heart had never felt freer. Jeopardy smiled at my bravery and offered me a cigarette. I refused but smiled back. So this was what it was like to be Jeopardy...carefree and adventurous! I had never been either of those things. No wonder Momma didn't like her; Momma wasn't carefree or adventurous either. But I loved my sister, and it felt good to see her smile. Even if it meant we were about to get into major trouble. I'd never done anything like this before, but it was too late to turn back now.

We held hands and ran all the way to the river.

Chapter Nine—Jerica

Something woke me from my dream, but I had no idea what it could have been. Nevertheless, I was wide awake and feeling quite perturbed. One minute I was running free with Harper and Jeopardy, an invisible witness to their family troubles, and the next I found myself staring up at a white painted ceiling. Sunlight filtered through sheer white curtains, and the sounds of birds surprised me. Oh, yes. Now I remembered. I was in Desire, and this was Summerleigh, or at least the cottage at Summerleigh. Imagine me, Jerica Poole, here in south Mississippi, the new owner of an old mansion.

My heart broke for Harper, but I needed to think about what I had seen. I wandered into the kitchen and hoped that Ben had been kind enough to have purchased coffee. He had! I would have to call him later and thank him. He'd really saved me by thinking ahead. Still, I would have to make that trip to the Piggly Wiggly in Lucedale sooner rather than later. As I loaded the filter and coffee into the white coffee machine, I thought about the silence. There were no sirens out here, no horns honking or rowdy neighbors yelling across balconies at one another. It was really like another world. A slower world.

While the machine sputtered to life, I sauntered upstairs to finish arranging my toiletries in the bathroom. I loved the fractured glass windows and the tidy tile job. The fixtures weren't showroom new, but who was I to look a gift horse in the mouth? And I had so much space. I arranged the towels and filled my medicine cabinet. My two missing prescriptions were a concern, but maybe I could postpone finding a new doctor awhile. After washing my face and brushing my teeth, I headed back down to grab that cup of coffee. My watch told me it was three o'clock. *That can't be right. Shoot. Don't tell me I killed another watch battery.* Watches and I never got along, but I had loved this one so much I figured I'd give it another shot. Well, maybe there was a battery place in town too.

I noticed for the first time that there was a squeak on the third stair down. That was slightly irritating. I would have to take a look at that. Might be just a loose board. As I checked out the suspect piece, I heard a light tapping on the back door. It was so light that I had to really focus to hear it. Yes, someone was here for sure.

"Coming!" I yelled, hoping it was JB. The back door was between the kitchen and the laundry room if I remembered correctly. I rubbed my eyes and wished I'd bothered to brush my hair. "Almost there," I said pleasantly. The clock on the wall told me it was eight. Man, I had slept late this morning. That never happened.

Unlocking the dead bolt, I opened the door with a friendly smile, but there was no one there. No one at all. "Hello?" I called out. No one answered, but arranged neatly on the bottom porch step was a small bouquet of flowers. Not the hothouse kind but wildflowers, purple, yellow and pink. The only one I recognized was the black-eyed Susans.

Marisol...

Who would have left these here? Someone very shy, apparently. Maybe JB had children or I had a neighbor closer than I thought? I hurried back inside and went to the kitchen. Grabbing a mason jar from the cabinet, I filled it with water and put the flowers in the window above the sink. Okay, I needed coffee. I sipped the black brew and enjoyed the flowers. It must have been one of JB's children who left them. Had to be. I didn't see any other houses around here. Trespassers didn't normally leave bouquets on your doorstep. I touched one flower and smiled at the sweet offering.

Now, what was my plan? For sure I needed a shower, but Summerleigh waited for my exploration. After another few swallows of hot coffee, I grabbed the keys and headed to the house. The cottage was about fifty yards from the main house, and it was a lovely morning for a walk. Instead of going through the back door, I opted to make it official and go around to the front. It all looked so familiar. Just like Harper showed me in my dream, just as she had described many times in our conversations.

"What a beautiful place, Harper," I said as I nearly tripped over a stone. What in the world? Who would put a marker this close to a pathway? Clearly, this wasn't some random rock but a stone marker with some inscription hidden under the grass. *That's funny*, I thought. The rest of the garden was so overgrown, that was true, but it had some order to it. This marker appeared to have been completely forgotten. Or at least overlooked. I squatted down and scooped away leaves. A tiny brown spider scurried away. Good thing too. Spiders were not my favorite creature.

In Loving Memory of a Lost Soul

Loving memory...so this was a person? I had thought perhaps a pet, but a person? This seemed an odd place for a memorial stone. How horribly sad.

Jeopardy! Could this be for Jeopardy Belle?

"Sorry, Jeopardy," I said as I lovingly touched the stone. And I didn't know why, but I added, "I'll bring you home...I promise." The wind fluttered my hair around me, and the sound of footsteps behind me made me stand up and look around. I saw no one.

I decided it was best not to linger here and allow my imagination to run away with me. I'd done that before, and look where that got me—medicated. I journeyed on to the house, walked to the welcoming front door and slid the key in. Some thoughtful person had wisely painted the porch floorboards a dark green. That was an excellent shade for hiding dirt and whatnot. I opened the front door and stepped inside Summerleigh for the first time. I remembered the mixed emotions Harper felt, and I experienced something similar. The porch and exterior had appeared so welcoming, except for the obvious roof disrepair, but there was nothing too welcome inside.

This would be what people would have called the Great Room when it was built. There was a sweeping staircase on the left side of the room that led to a windowed landing. Just before it and to the right were two evenly spaced wooden columns that gave you the feeling you'd stepped inside a Greek temple. In the center of the columns on the back wall was a large fireplace surrounded by built-in bookcases. *What a strange place to put a fireplace. Or maybe not. What do I know about south Mississippi architecture?* Not a lot, but I knew about wood. Whoever built this place spared no expense from what I could see, such beautiful oak and pine. Summerleigh must have been a beautiful place in her heyday, but happy? I had my doubts. I shivered again, wishing I had worn something besides shorts and a t-shirt.

To the left was an open door that presumably led to the kitchen and parlor. I remembered from Harper's time that the right side of the Great Room would lead to the bedrooms. At this moment, that area of the house felt dark and forbidding. Were the trees covering the windows? For a split second, I heard footsteps. I made the mistake of calling out, "Hello?" only to have the echo scare the snot out of me.

"Good Lord, Jerica. Get it together." I shoved the key in my pocket but decided to leave the door open. This place could use a good airing out. I went into the parlor; the faded burgundy area rug and matching couches were all too familiar. Only the radio was missing. I passed through the parlor and headed to the kitchen. As I stepped through the doorway, I had the urge to cry. Everything I had seen in the dream, the farm sink where Harper had filled the peach pot, the once shiny white stove, the family table, it had all been real. And because it was all real, the weight of my promise hit me hard. I was here to see justice done, not just for Jeopardy but for all the Belle girls. Yes, my dreams had all been real, and my promise!

Before I could take my thoughts to their expected conclusion, the front door slammed so hard the dishes in the kitchen cabinet shook. "Dear God!" I said as my knees buckled a second.

And then I heard footsteps.

A child's footsteps from the sound of them.

They were running up the stairs, and I took off after them.

Chapter Ten—Jerica

As I raced up the stairs and across the balcony, I paused briefly before clearing the last set of stairs. An entire unexplored floor stretched before me, but I was leery about adventuring too far from the staircase. Not because I was tired but because I had come to my senses. What was I doing chasing phantom footsteps across questionable flooring? And then the footsteps stopped just above me, and I heard the floorboards creak as if someone were standing on the top balcony looking down at me wondering why I was taking so long.

"Alright, just slow down," I said to no one in particular when I heard a whisper from above. I could tell it was a child's whisper, but for the life of me, I could not hear what she was saying. Was that a little girl? Or something that wanted me to think it was a girl?

With my pulse racing, I carefully climbed the last staircase and stood in the decrepit hallway. *Boy, this place hasn't seen any love in a long time.* The hallway wallpaper was in tatters, strips of the dry rotted paper had come off the walls in many places. There was a thick coat of dust on the floors and moldings. As I stood at the top, I counted four rooms on the top floor and a narrow door at the end of the hallway. Where did that go? The attic, of course— Jeopardy's castle room! "Hello?" I asked, praying that my own echo didn't come back in a frightening way. "Is anyone up here? I thought I heard...you."

Nothing. Not even a whisper now, but the air was electric as if I stood in a lightning storm that was ready to start popping at any moment. Then I heard a strange sound.

Thump. Click, click, click.

I waited and heard it again.

Thump. Click, click, click.

Off the top of my head, I couldn't say what that sound was, but it sounded familiar. I knew I'd heard it before. It was coming from the last room on the right. I passed the two empty rooms, one to my left and one to my right. There was no furniture up here and certainly no lost little girl. Maybe that was it? JB's kids? They liked to play in here. That had to be it. If this big old house stood empty, it seemed natural that some curious child or teenager might want to check it out. Funny, I hadn't seen any vandalism or other evidence of kids hanging out, no empty soda cans or candle stubs. Nothing except the flowers on my porch.

I now stood in the doorway of the largest room and waited. I couldn't make myself step into the room, not yet, but I heard the sound again. *Thump. Click, click...* I stepped inside expecting to see someone. Anyone. But I found a room that was empty except for an old wooden rocking horse, empty bookcases and a rolling red ball on the floor.

And a set of old metal jacks.

Oh, God, oh, God, oh, God! I immediately ran back down the hallway and cleared the staircases in a matter of seconds. The front door didn't want to open at first, but I kept tugging on it until it finally opened. Once I got into the yard I could breathe again.

That was the sound I heard! Someone was playing with the jacks. Loxley? Was Loxley's ghost here? *Oh, God! I can't do this.* I looked up at the empty window, but there was no one there. Wasn't that good? Did I want to see a ghost girl hanging out at the window?

Heck no. I walked around the house and headed for the caretaker's cottage. I had to think about this, or not think about it. I decided to get a shower after I locked the doors. Now was the perfect time to go to town. No sense in delaying my supply run. Thirty minutes later, the SUV was turning onto Highway 98 West. According to my GPS, Lucedale was only twenty minutes away. I could go to Mobile, but since JB had suggested the Piggly Wiggly to me, I thought I'd check it out.

I decided to take the town's Main Street and instantly fell in love with the charming little mom and pop shops that lined it. There was more than one shabby chic consignment furniture store (I'd have to check those out later for inspiration), a health food store, a clothing store, various specialty shops and a few restaurants. I liked it. After driving around for about ten minutes, I felt a bit disappointed that I hadn't found the Piggly Wiggly; however, there was another grocery store, as well as a big chain department store that had a grocery too. But now that my stomach was rumbling, I decided I'd rather stop at the diner I spotted, a little place called Ricky's Country Diner.

I pulled the SUV in and went inside to grab a bite to eat. Maybe someone in here would know how to get to the Piggly Wiggly. The place was packed. I hadn't expected that from the number of cars outside, but then again, some of these patrons were probably walk-ins. I found an empty table at the corner of the restaurant near the grill.

"Good morning. What can I get started for you?" This was no teeny-bopper waitress but a muscular man with intense dark eyes, dark hair and a deep voice speaking to me. I had not expected him either.

"Um, I have no idea." I handled a laminated menu but couldn't narrow down my choices. "It's my first time here. What do you suggest?"

"It's pretty close to breakfast, and we're still serving. The breakfast platter is a winner. The most popular dish is the Double Slam. How do you like your eggs?"

"Over medium."

He nodded. "And what to drink, ma'am?"

"Orange juice, please."

"Alright, I'll get that started."

I couldn't help but watch him walk away. *Wow, he's...*

"I know, he's a bit of eye candy, isn't he? But don't let that body fool you. Jesse Clarke has more brains than most. Hi, I'm Renee, but my friends call me Ree-Ree. Jesse is my cousin; we own this restaurant. You're a new face. First time here?" She smiled politely.

"Hi, Renee, Ree-Ree. I'm Jerica. Yes, first time here. I wasn't staring. It's just I wasn't expecting to see..."

"Oh, no need to apologize. Everyone stares at Jesse...he's just that handsome. Just passing through? Headed to Leakesville, maybe?" Without an invitation, Renee sat in the chair opposite me. I didn't mind, but I was a bit surprised. She got busy wrapping silverware, a fancy task for a small diner such as this one.

I smiled politely but hoped to change the direction of this conversation. I hated that I got busted ogling the waiter. "No, I live in Desire now. I was told that the Piggly Wiggly was a good place for groceries, but I'm kind of lost."

"Lost in Lucedale?" She chuckled and finished up her silverware, depositing the last one in a plastic tub. "And there's no Piggly Wiggly here anymore. Hasn't been in about five years, I'm guessing. Hey, Humble. When did the Piggly Wiggly leave?"

"2012," an old man answered her. He hardly missed a bite of his food.

"Yeah, that's what I thought. 2012. Someone sent you on a wild goose chase, Jerica. But we do have a

Wayne Lee's. And of course, there's the big blue store that everyone hates but goes to anyway. What were you drinking?"

"Oh, orange juice."

"Be right back." Renee had long dark hair that she wore in a tight ponytail at the back of her head. She wore plenty of makeup, especially black mascara, but she didn't really need any of it. She had lovely skin, like her cousin Jesse. I stole another peek at him as she returned with my drink. He was actually the cook, not just the waiter. I guessed it made sense since he was one of the owners. He caught me staring, and I pretended to look at the menu. *Good Lord, Jerica. You're not a teenager.*

"Here you go. So, you rode over from Desire? Not much left of that little town, if you could ever call it that. Did you know that their old downtown area is nothing but a ghost town now? I guess you've seen it. Just three or four empty old buildings. Kudzu vines all over the place. It's sad. Where you staying, on the river? They've got some cute fishing cabins over there."

"I've never been fishing," I confessed. "I'm actually staying at Summerleigh."

"Summerleigh?" I couldn't help but notice that a few eyes were on me now. Including Renee's wide brown ones. "Why would you stay there? That place is..." I thought she was going to say haunted, but she caught herself and said, "falling down."

"Actually, I'm in the caretaker's cottage, but I do have plans to fix up the house. It's not that bad inside, but it does need some repairs to the flooring for a start. Do you know a good handyman? I have some skills with a saw, but I could use an extra pair of hands on this project." Jesse arrived with my breakfast plate, two eggs, bacon and a pile of grits with a biscuit. My stomach rumbled at the sight. I didn't often eat grits, but these looked delicious. "Thank you," I said.

"You're welcome."

Renee blurted out, "This is Jerica, and she's staying at Summerleigh."

Jesse wasn't impressed, but he didn't sound surprised either. "You plan on restoring it?"

"Yes, I do. I would like to make some basic repairs to start with. I promised Harper I would tend to a few things. I guess you know she passed away."

Renee shook her head at hearing the news. "I hadn't heard that. How sad. That whole Belle family, such a sad ending for all of them. But then again, I guess you'd expect that. They were a wild lot, by all accounts. Wait, are you a Belle?"

"Oh no, I'm not. Just a friend of Harper's."

"Shoot. Looks like Humble is ready to go. I'll go check him out. Hey, Jesse, she's looking for a handyman. Might be one way to get your boat fixed. You'll never make the money you need slinging eggs here."

Renee excused herself, but her cousin lingered. "That true? You need some help up at Summerleigh?" He tossed a semi-clean white rag in his hands a few times before he slung it over his broad shoulder.

"Mostly carpentry work to begin with. As I was telling your cousin, I know how to work a saw, but it would be nice to have an extra pair of hands. I wouldn't want to take you away from your work here, though."

"What work? Carpentry is my second love."

"Oh, what's your first?" I asked curiously. "Cooking?"

"No. I'm just filling in for Norman. That would be writing. I've done quite a bit of research on Summerleigh and the disappearance of Jeopardy Belle."

"Really?"

"Yes, but I should let you eat your food before it gets cold. I've got a few orders to cook."

"Um, okay," I said, totally curious about his research on Jeopardy. "Why don't you ride up to the house later? Maybe take a look at what I'm talking about. It's a pretty big job, and I'd feel better if you knew what you were in for." *And I'd feel better if you could show me you could actually handle a board.*

"Sounds great. I get off at three if that's okay."

"Great, I'm in the caretaker's cottage in the back. You can't miss it."

"I'll be there about four. I'd like to get the aroma of food off me first."

"Four it is, thanks."

As he walked away, I didn't question what I was doing. Even if he wasn't interested in the work, I was interested in him. I mean, interested in his information.

I ate a few bites of my plate and left. I had a lot to do before four o'clock.

Chapter Eleven—Jerica

When I opened the door, I was surprised to see that I had two visitors standing on my doorstep. Before I could greet either of them, Renee waved and said, "Surprise! I couldn't let him come without me. I'm dying to see the place. I hope that's okay."

"Sure, the more the merrier. Come in, please."

I was glad I'd opted for jeans and a fresh t-shirt instead of that sundress. This was supposed to be a business meeting, not a date. But Jesse Clarke was even better looking without his stained apron. He too wore blue jeans and a soft t-shirt. *Get it together, Jerica.*

"Do you guys want something to drink? I have some tea made."

"None for me," Jesse and Renee said almost simultaneously.

"Let me get the key and we can take a look at the house." *Well, this wasn't how I thought things would go, but hey, I guess you have to learn to roll with the punches. Does Renee think her cousin needs a bodyguard or something?*

I grabbed the keys off the rack, and we left the cottage behind. I made it a point to show them the memorial stone. "I nearly tripped over this yesterday. Any ideas what this stone is for? I assume for Jeopardy Belle, but I can't be sure."

Renee shivered in the sunlight. "I don't know. What do you think, Jesse?"

"Could be." He squatted down and examined the stone closer, rubbing the concrete. "Doesn't look all that old, as far as monuments go. I guess it could be for Jeopardy, but then again, there's been a lot of tragedy here—even a murder or two, with the Belles and the McIntyre family before that." He got up, and the three of us continued on toward Summerleigh. Like my earlier trip, I decided to go around to the front of the house. Going through the back door felt like I was intruding.

"Who was murdered? One of the Belles?"

"Nobody knows what happened to Jeopardy; she disappeared in the summer of 1942, not long after her father died. That was a tragedy, but the murder I mentioned was Mariana McIntyre. She lived here long before the Belles, in the late 1800s. She died on her sixteenth birthday. The story goes, she went upstairs to change gowns during her birthday party. When she missed her grand entrance, someone went up to check on her and found her dead. Someone had cut off all her hair and stabbed her with her own sewing scissors. It was a gory murder, and quite shocking for 1870s Desire, Mississippi. So shocking that the town almost folded after that. Then Bull McIntyre, that was Mariana's father, had a stroke. Not long after that, he died too. Mariana's younger brother inherited the place, but he went crazy. Gosh, I can't remember his name. Bull McIntyre had been the mayor of Desire, but there was a lot of speculation about his role in his daughter's death. The place stood empty for a while, then it was sold a few times, but nobody really tried to make it a home until John Belle won Summerleigh in a poker game."

"I heard the story about how he won this place," I said with a laugh. "He must have had quite a hand."

"Full house, from what I hear."

"You know quite a lot about the house. Have you ever been inside?"

"Yes, but not legally."

Renee touched my arm. "He wrote a book about this place. If you ever want to know anything about Summerleigh, he's the guy to ask. Jesse is obsessed with old houses. And not just this one."

"Well, here we go." My mind was full of bloody scenes. To think, a girl had been murdered in this house, and then not a century later, another vanished. Maybe it was the house.

I opened the door and we stepped inside. It felt better in here now, although the staleness hadn't improved. I didn't hear any footsteps, thankfully, but I wasn't any more comfortable than I had been earlier. As if the dust knew I had a thing for it, I started sneezing.

"Bless you," Jesse said.

"Thanks. This dust has me sneezing my head off."

"Ugh, that's a horrible thing to say in this house," Renee said.

I blushed. "Sorry."

Jesse strolled around and examined the flooring. "The flooring in this room looks pretty good. Have you been under the house?"

"No, I have a thing about spiders," I confessed with an awkward shrug.

"I can do it. Which floors are you concerned with the most?"

"I think the parlor just to the left here might have some issues, and the upper balcony and some of the stair treads need replacing." I walked toward the parlor with Jesse in tow, but Renee was walking the other way. "You coming, Renee?"

"If you don't mind, may I wander around? I won't touch anything."

"Um, sure."

Jesse shook his head and said in a low voice, "Renee thinks she's some sort of psychic. I guess I should have left her at the diner, but she really wanted to come. This place is kind of a curiosity to the locals. Not many folks have been inside. Your friend Harper was pretty protective of the place."

"Psychic, huh? I wouldn't have thought that, but then again, I've never met a psychic before."

"You'll find the Clarke family a strange bunch. Hey, I see what you mean." He looked up at the ceiling. "Yeah, looks like you might have had a leak at one time."

"Sure, that makes sense. I noticed the roof damage when I drove up but didn't put the two together. So, roof first over here and then the floor. I don't suppose you can do roofs too."

"No, but I know an excellent roofer. With all the summer storms we have down here, you learn to have a roofer on speed dial."

Hearing footsteps again, I glanced at the door. "You sure she's okay?"

"Yeah, what about the kitchen?"

"Alright."

We went from room to room and found plenty of things that needed the attention of a few competent pairs of hands. By the sound of it, Jesse Clarke knew what he was talking about. There was evidence of rodents in the kitchen, the parlor floor was damaged, and some of the windows in the west wing needed replacing before they fell out. "It's all lead paint, anyway. They'll have to be cleaned and repainted. But overall, I'm surprised there's not much more damage. It's never good for a house to sit empty. I don't mean to be nosy, and I'm not trying to discourage you—God knows I need the work—but are you sure you're up for this? This is going to be one helluva project, and a long one, not to mention expensive."

"One step at a time was my Dad's motto. Mine too. I'm willing to try."

He smiled, but it didn't last long. I could see that Jesse was more on the serious side. "That's all I need to hear. Let's check out the upstairs."

"Did I hear your cousin say you own a boat?"

"No, I own the hull of a boat. I have plenty of work ahead of me. Just like we do here."

I tucked my hair behind my ear, suddenly very conscious that I had skimped on my makeup and hair care today.

Renee met us on the stairs; her face was pale, and her worried expression bothered me. "I'll be in the truck, Jess."

"What's wrong? You look like you've seen..."

"I have, and I don't want to see another one. I'll be in the truck." We both stared at her as she walked out of the house and slammed the door behind her.

"Um, should we go after her?"

"No. Like I said, Jerica, we're a weird bunch." For the first time today, he used my name. I liked hearing that. "Is this the floor?" Neither one of us talked about ghosts, and I didn't hear any jacks or footsteps, thankfully. We finished our tour of the house and walked to the front porch. Did I really want to work so closely with someone I didn't really know? Jesse was right, this was going to be an expensive project. I mean, Harper had been very generous, but it wouldn't be hard to drop that hundred grand here. I'd been so shocked to receive the life insurance check in the mail. I'd never imagined Harper would make me her sole heir! Again, the responsibility of it all weighed on me. Yes, I had to be wise about this. One step at a time, I reminded myself.

"Well, let's start with the roofer. If you could call him and maybe have him come out Monday? I hate to get anything started at the end of the week. Then we'll start on the parlor floors. Let's get the bottom floor tended to and work our way up. What are your hours? I'll be happy to work around them."

"I'm all yours. I mean..." He cleared his throat. "I mean I was only helping out at the diner temporarily. I'm an owner, but I don't work there all the time. I can go at this full time if you need me."

"Let's start Monday, eight o'clock. We'll see what the roofer has to say and go from there."

"That sounds like a plan. Hey, I'm playing at a benefit tomorrow night at the Community Center in Lucedale. Why don't you come out and meet some of the locals?" We walked down off the porch and stepped into the hot sunshine.

"Maybe, what time?"

"Starts at seven. It's a fish fry for a young lady who needs medical funding. A friend of the family."

"I might surprise you," I said with a smile. "Thanks for the invite." We went back to my cottage and found Renee sweating in the truck.

"Renee, you could have waited in the caretaker's cottage," I said. "It's too hot to wait out in the heat."

"I'm okay. I just want to go home."

Jesse frowned at her but cranked up the truck. Before I could ask her anything else, she rolled up the window and the truck lumbered away.

As they passed the corner of Summerleigh, Jesse turned his head my way and waved once, and I waved back.

That's when I saw Ann standing at the kitchen window. She didn't look happy to see me. I ran into the cottage and locked the door.

Chapter Twelve—Harper

Daddy's homecoming parties had always brought the Belle family together, until this one. Momma didn't cook Daddy's favorite dishes. Aunt Dot was unofficially banned from Summerleigh, at least until Momma said otherwise. No one from the church called to inquire about any party for Daddy—usually, some of the First Baptist ladies came by to bring a dessert or something. Even Miss Augustine begged off tonight citing the horrible weather, which was strange because Momma left early in the afternoon in the Master DeLuxe. I thought for sure she was spending the day with Miss Augustine, maybe going to the beauty shop before Daddy got home. And now it looked like she hadn't even gone to the bus station to pick him up. Someone must have dropped him off at the road. At long last, he walked up to the house, arriving drenched and grim-faced. If I had known he needed a ride home, I would have ventured out on the road myself in his old truck. I'd faithfully cranked it for him every week, just like he'd asked me to in his one and only letter to me.

Loxley opened the front door wide and danced on the porch as he approached. "Daddy's home! Daddy's home!" Addison and I clapped our hands too. The three of us couldn't stop smiling. Yes, Daddy was home, and all would be right again.

All would be right!

I looked around for Jeopardy; she was normally the first one out the door. At previous homecoming celebrations, she would declare, "I'm the oldest," as she grabbed Daddy's hand first, but she was no-where to be found this evening. I knew she was here, probably creeping around in the attic. She'd taken to staying up there. Even though I took a belt for going with her to the river, it had been worth it. I'd seen a whole other side of my sister. She was popular and smiling when she was with her rebellious crowd, and there wasn't a boy there that didn't call her name or whistle at her when she splashed around in the water. Even Troy Harvester made goo-goo eyes at her, but she acted like he wasn't even there. That was strange because she used to kiss her pillow like a movie star and call his name to make me laugh. I knew she liked him. Or she used to.

"Jeopardy," I called once before I helped Daddy bring his bags inside. I couldn't imagine why she'd miss this. Addison helped me carry his things in while Loxley climbed up into his wet arms and cried.

"No crying now, and you'll be wet through if you don't let me change my clothes. Where's your mother? I waited for her for hours."

"She left this morning," Addison said as she wiped at her nose. I closed the door before she got sick again. "We thought she was bringing you home."

He kissed each one of us on the top of our heads and removed his hat before he went to the phone. He made a few calls, but nobody seemed to know where Momma had gotten to. I couldn't hide my worried expression. There was so much I wanted to tell Daddy, but now I just couldn't.

"Where's Jeopardy? Did she go with your mother?"

"No, Daddy, I think she's upstairs."

His smile disappeared, and he kissed me on the top of the head again. He glanced up at the ceiling and then said quietly, "Addison and Loxley, do you think you two could manage to haul my bag to my room? It's very heavy now and very wet."

"Yes, Daddy." They beamed and scrambled out the door to make Daddy's wish come true.

"What's happening, Harper? Are you girls okay?"

A fat tear fell on my cheek, and I pawed it away as I fell into Daddy's arms. I didn't care that his clothing smelled damp and sweaty. Everything tumbled out of my mouth at once. I told him about the falling out between Aunt Dot and Momma, about Momma and Jeopardy fighting at church and...I even told him about the few nights that Momma slipped out when she thought we were all asleep. I told him more than I should have; I could tell by the way his jaw popped when he looked at me.

"Daddy, are you going to stay home now? Please, stay home."

He hugged me tightly but didn't give me the answer I wanted. "Harper Belle, I love you. It's going to be alright. I need you to be strong just a while longer. You think you could do that?"

"Yes, Daddy."

"You got something in the fridge you could heat up for supper? I'm hungry, and it's been a long time since I ate anything."

I thought about it for a minute and wiped the tears away. "Yes, sir. There is some rice and gravy left over from supper. I can make you some biscuits too."

"No biscuits. Rice and gravy is plenty. Did you girls eat yet?"

"Yes, sir. I made the rice and gravy."

His jaw popped again. "I'm going up to see your sister. I'll be back for that delicious meal. Thank you, Harper." I loved how Daddy always treated me like a grown-up. Always. Even when I was really little, he talked to me like I was big. And now I was.

I heard Daddy's footsteps on the stairs as he went up to see Jeopardy. I couldn't help but be nosy. I snuck to the bottom of the stairs and waited to see what kind of welcome he got. She'd been so moody lately, so angry at me. Maybe now that our father was home, she'd feel better about Momma, Addison and Loxley. And me.

My two little sisters caught me spying, but they didn't tell on me. They waited too. We heard Jeopardy crying her heart out. Loxley smiled up at me, her blue eyes moist, her lips quivering. "Daddy's home now, Harper."

"Yes, he is. Why don't you two help me get his supper ready? Daddy needs food and lots of it. He's been fighting the enemy, and he's probably really hungry."

"I'll help!" Loxley ran into the kitchen first and began to set the table. Addison arranged a jar full of wildflowers in front of his plate. I'd seen her out picking them earlier. It had been nice to see her out of doors, even though I worried that she'd get sick afterward. So far, so good. I smiled when I noticed she had a healthy pink glow in her cheeks. She smiled back. I poured a tiny amount of water in the saucepan to heat up the rice and poured the gravy into a smaller pan. There were also fresh peaches, so Addison and I peeled some and tossed them with sugar and cinnamon for Daddy's dessert. We were beginning to wonder if he'd ever come downstairs when we heard Momma's Master DeLuxe pull into the drive. Addison's eyes widened, and Loxley sat quietly in her chair as the back door opened. Momma walked in with shopping bags in her arms. She deposited the wet paper bags on the counter and peeled off her rain hat and coat. It was then that she noticed Daddy's hat on the table. She didn't say a word, but the smile vanished from her face as she hung up her coat on one of the hooks behind the door. She must have forgotten all about Daddy's homecoming.

"Loxley, go wash your face. Addison, how are you feeling, dear? Your cheeks are so pink." She laid the back of her hand on Addison's forehead and clucked once. "I hope that's not a fever you have coming on." Addison sniffed in response and touched her own forehead. "Harper, cat got your tongue?"

"Girls, go upstairs." Daddy was in the doorway now. I flicked off the burners and glanced at Momma, and in that moment she knew. She knew I'd betrayed her and told Daddy her secret. She knew I'd told Daddy everything. And what had Jeopardy told him? "Now, Harper."

"Yes, sir," I whispered as I exited with my sisters. We did as he told us and scrambled up the stairs, at least as far as the landing. We could hear dishes breaking in the kitchen and furniture getting slung about. Momma screamed at Daddy and called him a name we were all forbidden to use. Daddy's voice rose, but not as high as hers, and as far as I could tell, she wasn't getting the best of him.

"How could...Ann...I'm never...police...now!"

"I didn't know...JB...I swear..."

They continued to quarrel, and Daddy was in the Great Room now, Momma running behind him. Clearly, he wanted to leave again. "You'll shame her if you do that, John. You'll shame her in front of everyone."

"The shame is on you!" He stomped out of the house and slammed the front door with a big boom. I heard his old truck crank up, and soon Daddy was gone. All of us were crying now. Momma didn't come up to see us or check on us. Nobody went downstairs again that night. We didn't know what to do. Momma was crying pitifully, and a part of me wanted to comfort her too, but right now I had to think of Addison and Loxley...and Jeopardy.

"Come on, Belles. Let's go see if Jeopardy will let us in." We walked down the long hallway and tapped on the attic door. "Please let us in, Jeopardy. Daddy is gone, and we don't want to go downstairs."

She opened the door, her face a swollen mess, her hair a pile of tangles. She'd been crying, but at least she didn't look at me like she hated me. She stepped back and let us into her sanctuary. *So this was where all the spare blankets and pillows had gone to.* Who all was sleeping up here? Nobody talked. We were all confused, it seemed. All disappointed that Daddy had left us. All except Jeopardy. She was almost peaceful as she lit a candle for us and then a cigarette for herself and dropped the matchstick in an empty soda bottle. Nobody scolded her. We all found a place to lie down and waited for Daddy to come back.

That's where Aunt Dot found us the following morning; a tangle of arms and legs, all of us Belles sleeping on one big pallet. And then she told us the horrible news. Daddy was dead, hit by another vehicle on Bloody Highway 98. The rainy roads had kept anyone from finding him until it was too late. He'd bled out and was gone.

The day after we buried him was the first time Loxley saw his ghost.

None of the rest of us ever saw Daddy again.

Chapter Thirteen—Jerica

Arms were around my neck, sweet, young arms. They hugged me tight, and I felt the lightest whisper of a kiss on my cheek. My hand went to brush her hair, as I always did, but she slid away from me. My eyes blinked open, and I saw that I was alone. Again.

It took a few moments for the heartbreak to come, but it did not fail to arrive. And with it came the realization that my Marisol would never hug me again.

Marisol...baby girl.

And I remembered the horrible dream—the complete and utter loss of John Jeffrey Belle. Harper's loss. It would be something she never got over. I could feel that now.

Oh my God! This was JB—John Jeffrey Belle was the very same man I met when I came to Summerleigh.

He was no gardener but a ghost! Was he the one who left me the flowers? No. That was something a child would do, not a grown man. Not a tough hero like John Belle. I sat up on the bed trying to wrap my head around it all. And how was any of this getting me closer to finding Jeopardy Belle? Why was my daughter here? I swung the quilt back and decided there was no time like the present to get started on my mission. I'd fallen in love with this place. I wanted to see Summerleigh restored, not just for me but for Harper and all the Belle girls, but that act would be empty without finding Jeopardy and bringing her home to Desire. Where to get started? I'd pick Jesse's brain later; he seemed like a guy who knew quite a bit about local lore. But in the meantime, I was going to that potting shed to find out for myself if the man I had seen was actually Harper's father. What would my therapist say about all this?

Ghosts aren't real, Jerica. They are extensions of us, our emotions, unresolved feelings, but they aren't real. Marisol is gone, and you have to forgive yourself. Let her go.

And that had been the last time I'd seen Dr. Busby. What was the point? He didn't believe me when I told him I saw Marisol. I knew I wasn't responsible for my daughter's death, but I think for some strange reason Dr. Busby believed otherwise. I knew for a fact Eddie blamed me. Yes, I'd been in the car when the train hit us, when the metal twisted and my baby screamed for her mother. That had been me, but I had done all I could do. It wasn't my fault that the truck behind me pushed us onto the tracks. I smothered a sob and forced myself to keep moving.

Keep moving, Jerica.

I recognized this feeling. Not only was I knee-deep in grief again, but I was coming down with something. Hopefully not the flu. I didn't mind taking care of others but had no patience for being sick myself. I simply had too much to do.

I threw on some work clothes and my beat-up tennis shoes. With a heavy heart, I headed outside to look for the potting shed. Taking the gravel path to the left of the cottage seemed intuitive, so I followed it around and found a dilapidated shack not far in the distance. As I cleared a copse of trees and stood before a small potting shed, my heart sank. Windows were missing, many windows. A tattered blue tarp hung from the side of the roof, a clear indication that this building was probably now in complete disrepair. With a sigh, I opened the door and stepped inside. My heart sank even further when I saw that the shelves held nothing more than pots of old soil, weeds and rusty gardening tools. Nobody was here, and nobody had been here for a very long time.

"JB? Are you here?"

I stood in the middle of the potting shed, my hair crackling on my neck. And as each moment passed, the feeling that someone watched me intensified. I asked again, "JB? John Jeffrey Belle? Are you here?"

No one answered. Did I expect him to pipe up and say, "Yes, I'm over here?" Not really, but then again Summerleigh had proved to be a kind of magical place in that regard. As I walked around the shed, I was discouraged by the shape it was in but found an interesting book half hidden in a clod of dirt on a rickety potting table. *Neat handwriting*, I thought as I held a page up to the light to read the faded pencil markings better. A former gardener, possibly John Belle, had taken the time to write down the names of plants, the days they had been planted and other notations only a plant lover would understand. I flipped to the back of the book for more clues and was surprised to see that it didn't belong to John Belle after all. This book had clearly belonged to a

McIntyre. I squinted at the first name but couldn't make it out.

Interesting bit of history. I'm sure Jesse would love to see this.

The laughter of little girls brought me back to the present. I ran to the window in front of me. The glass was broken, and I was careful not to place my hands in any of the panes. I almost fell to the ground when I saw the back of two girls clearing a group of trees in front of me, one with blond braids and the other with brown hair, like mine.

Marisol! Like a madwoman, I ran down the path after them. "Marisol! Wait!"

I heard the pair giggling again and even detected footsteps on the gravel not far ahead of me, but I could not catch up with them. No matter how fast I ran, they ran faster. Marisol and Loxley—that had certainly been Loxley—were always just out of my reach. I didn't realize how far back I had traveled onto the property, but I had managed to navigate my way to the banks of a river. Was this Dog River? I'd read that this was a tributary of the Escatawpa, but I couldn't be sure.

I traveled the banks for a while, walking up and down. I found evidence that this had once been a popular party place, but solid footprints of two little girls were nonexistent.

"Don't let this be my imagination. Not again! I can't do this again!"

As if she heard me, Marisol peeked her head around the trunk of a live oak tree. My hands flew to my mouth as I muffled a surprised yelp. I whispered her name, but she just smiled and vanished. I raced to the tree, but my daughter had disappeared. The sound of footsteps running away told me I would not catch up with her. Nor did she want me to, for some reason. I collapsed under the tree and cried my eyes out. I cried like I hadn't cried in two years. *Why is this happening now?* When I finished my crying jag, I got up and wiped my sweaty face with the back of my hand and walked back to Summerleigh.

I had things to do today, and it was looking less likely that I would make it to Jesse's benefit. I couldn't trust my emotions, and I was pretty certain a serious bug had a hold of me. After hiking back, I spent the next hour arranging my meager belongings in the caretaker's cottage and then took my camera and headed to the main house.

I had already seen the ghost of my child, so what else was there to be afraid of? I was going to go inside and explore every inch of Summerleigh. I was a woman on a mission. I had to find Jeopardy Belle. If I found her, maybe Marisol would stay. Why else would she be here but to encourage me in my search?

As I walked through the yard to the back of the house, I said aloud, "I'm coming, Jeopardy. I won't let you down."

Chapter Fourteen—Harper

Momma insisted that we eat dinner together at the supper table tonight. I couldn't think why. My sisters and I had been living off sandwiches or dishes prepared by various church ladies for the past month since Daddy's passing. For the first week after the funeral, Momma had kept to her room, crying night and day. Like all of us...except Jeopardy, who didn't cry at all anymore. I knew her heart was breaking; I'd heard her crying the night after Daddy died, but nothing since. Even Aunt Dot tried to talk with her, but she wouldn't speak about Daddy. Or anything, really. The only thing she did was sneak out of the house, smoke her stolen cigarettes in the potting shed and draw or doodle on paper. Once, I saw her shove a note into a chink in the attic wall, but she wasn't pleased that I'd spied on her; when I snuck back to read it, the note was gone.

She did strange things nowadays like wear bright lipstick and smudge mascara on her eyes. Momma never said a word to her, but she noticed. I could see her raise her eyebrows, though she said nothing. Feeling inspired, I dabbed on some of Momma's palest pink lipstick one afternoon and got the back of her hand on my mouth. "Isn't one whore in this family enough?" she asked me as I lay sprawled out on the ground.

I never wore lipstick again. Not as long as she was alive.

Miss Augustine had cooked tonight's supper, chicken and dressing. It was loaded with onions and I hated every bite, but who knew when we would eat again? Even picky Addison swallowed a few bites. Momma surveyed us all between her neat spoons of food.

Loxley ate like a hungry bear when she wasn't giggling at something, something or someone none of the rest of us could see.

"What in the world is so funny, Loxley Grace?"

Her eyes widened as she focused her attention on Momma now. "Nothing, Momma," was her sweet answer. It was an obvious lie, as she continued to giggle and spew Miss Augustine's horrible corn-bread dressing everywhere.

"What do you see?" Jeopardy asked as she leaned next to Loxley.

Loxley didn't speak but played with her food.

"Yes, Loxley. Who are you making such faces at? If it's that funny, I want to know too." Momma's sweetest voice was always a trap that Loxley fell into. I tried to kick her under the table as a warning but missed. Addison yelped in pain.

"Sorry," I muttered.

"Daddy. Daddy is making funny faces, and he makes me laugh."

Only Jeopardy smiled.

Momma rose to her feet, and Loxley shrank down in her chair. "You stop telling lies, Loxley Grace! Go to your room. No more supper for you."

She snatched my sister's plate away, and the youngest Belle practically crawled out of the room. Momma put the near-empty plate in the sink and stared out the window into the dusky Mississippi evening. Fireflies were bouncing around already, and some of them hit the window. They looked like fairies that wanted permission to come inside. I could see them clearly.

When Momma spoke again, it was a strange sound, like measured steel. "Jeopardy, Dr. Leland wants some of those jars of peaches we have in the laundry room. You take him three or four after supper. See that he pays you, though. At least a dollar a jar."

Jeopardy's fork hit her plate, and her eyes narrowed.

A dollar a jar? Who in their right mind would pay a dollar a jar for some peaches?

"It's almost dark, Momma. Can't she go in the morning?" Addison asked nervously. Addie hated the dark and still slept with the lamp on every chance she got. She didn't like the idea of any of us being in the dark now. Hadn't Daddy died venturing out in the dark?

Jeopardy crossed her bare arms and said, "No."

Momma turned around and put her hands behind her on the sink. She looked perfect, like a catalog model, but right at that moment, I knew something was wrong with her. She was like a mannequin, perfect to look at but without a soul. Yes, that was it. Her soul was gone. Or something.

"I'll go, Momma. I'm not afraid of the dark, and I can walk really fast. I don't mind going for Jeopardy," I offered as an alternative.

Momma smiled at Jeopardy. "Should I let your sister go instead?"

Jeopardy was on her feet now. "You wouldn't send her. You wouldn't dare!"

Momma's left eyebrow lifted slightly, but she never shifted her gaze from Jeopardy's pinched face. "Wouldn't I?"

Jeopardy threw her plate on the floor, and cornbread splattered all over the tile. Addison crept out of her chair and stood by the door that led to the parlor. I couldn't move. *What do I do? Daddy? Are you here?*

"You can't do that! You wouldn't do that!"

"I would too. You do what I tell you, Jeopardy. We need the money."

Jeopardy slammed her chair under the table and stalked into the pantry to retrieve a few jars of peaches. She stuffed them in a cloth bag we kept hanging next to Momma's purse and keys.

"Can't we drive over there and drop them off? I could take Daddy's truck," I offered as one last idea to avoid whatever disaster lay ahead of us.

"No, we don't have the gas for that. Jeopardy can take the peaches; you clean up this mess, Harper." Momma lit a cigarette as the screen door slapped closed. Jeopardy was gone. I obediently cleaned up the mess while I smothered my tears. Momma left the kitchen to listen to Amanda of Honeymoon Hill on the stand-up radio.

It got dark fast. By the time I dried the last dish, it was well after eight and there was no sign of my sister. I snuck Loxley a sandwich and a glass of milk before I went in to bed.

I waited up for Jeopardy, hoping to hear that she was safe and sound, but my tired eyes let me down. I closed them only for a moment. And when I opened them again, the sun was up and Loxley was sleeping beside me.

I wondered if Jeopardy ever made it home. No one else was awake except Momma, who was busy putting on her face. I could hear her humming to herself like she always did when she got dressed in the mornings. I'd have to cook breakfast soon, but I had enough time to slip upstairs. Whether Jeopardy liked it or not, I was going to invade her castle.

The door wasn't locked. I didn't have to knock or beg for permission to come in. Jeopardy was there, sleeping in nothing but her slip. I gasped at the sight of her. From head to toe, Jeopardy was covered in bruises.

She never opened her eyes, but she must have detected I was there. "Get out, Harper."

"Jeopardy, what happened to you? Did you fall in a ravine?"

She finally opened her eyes and said something I would never forget as long as I lived. "The devil got a hold of me, Harper Belle. He put his hands all over me. Now get out." She rolled over and turned her back to me. I wanted to hug her, help her, but I could see it would do no good. She would talk to me when she was ready to and not until then.

As I went downstairs to cook breakfast, I couldn't help but think about what she said. What could that mean?

The devil got a hold of me, Harper Belle...

Chapter Fifteen—Harper

Addison and Loxley played a hand-clapping game on the front porch. It was a familiar song, Miss Mary Mack. Loxley did all the singing because Addison had a sore throat, but even the littlest Belle knew to keep things toned down today. The quiet tension rose, and it didn't help that Jeopardy was stomping around upstairs; I could hear her footsteps as I passed through the Great Room. Fortunately, no one else had yet.

Momma lounged in the parlor with Miss Augustine. The two of them were flipping through magazines and gossiping about Bette Davis' new movie, The Man Who Came to Dinner. They'd driven all the way to Mobile twice to see it, and both times came back with something negative to say about the big-eyed actress. According to Desire's cultural department, the two women in our parlor, Bette Davis was a sourpuss with no acting skills whatsoever. I tried not to snort. I'd never seen a Bette Davis movie, but since these two didn't like her, I figured I probably would.

And the debate raged on. Lana Turner was hands down Momma's favorite, while Miss Augustine preferred Rita Hayworth or Gene Tierney. "Lana Turner is too hoity-toity for my taste." The two women rarely argued about anything except important matters like who should get top billing in Hollywood's latest film or which actress had the most beautiful penmanship or some other nonsense they'd fight to the death to have the last word about. Before Daddy left us, Momma used to teach Loxley how to walk and wave properly, just in case she landed a pageant, but not anymore. Loxley didn't seem to mind. Momma used to win pageants when she was young. Lots of them.

"Really, Ann. You go too far!"

Today was one of those days. Miss Augustine made an offhand remark about someone's bathing suit photos in the tabloids, and Momma exploded. Luckily for Miss Augustine, Momma took her home and didn't make her walk, but our mother came back in an even greater huff than the one she left in. Everyone got quiet when her car pulled into the driveway. We waited for her inner storm to abate, all except Jeopardy. She kept walking around upstairs, and a few times I thought I heard her talking to herself. Once Momma got settled into her chair again, I said, "The Lady Detective Show is coming on. Should we listen to it?" Addison clapped her hands gleefully and came in off the porch, to which Loxley made a raspberry sound at her back. I noticed she came inside too, though. Momma's eyes went to the ceiling; she must have heard Jeopardy, but she didn't care enough to ask about her. But then someone knocked at the front door.

After fussing with her hair for a moment, Momma went to the door with all us girls except one trailing behind her. I couldn't believe who was standing there, complete with a bouquet of flowers in his shaking hands.

It was Troy Harvester, looking nice and smiling nervously at Momma. "Good afternoon, Mrs. Belle. I'm here to see Jeopardy, if I may."

Addison gave me a wide-eyed look, which I answered with a shrug. To my surprise, Jeopardy came down the stairs and paused at the bottom. It was clear she didn't know Troy was coming. For the first time in a long time, I saw Jeopardy's cryptic smile appear on her narrow face. Her cheeks turned pink, but she didn't come any closer. She wore her pink romper today, the one that had the cherries at the bosom. It was really too small for her, showing way too much leg. In fact, I remembered Momma telling her to hand it down to Addison, but she never did. She liked it, and the pink color made her tanned legs look long and slender, or so she said. I was definitely too tall for such a thing.

Jeopardy stood on the bottom step and leaned her back against the wall. She didn't come to the door or act like she cared at all that Troy was here, but I knew she cared. She always cared about Troy.

"I know why you're here. You came sniffing. Boys like you always do. Get out of here now! Before I call your mother and tell her..."

"Hey!" Jeopardy yelled as she rushed toward the door. "You can't send my friend away. He came to see me."

Momma simultaneously slammed the front door and slapped Jeopardy to the ground. "You little whore! So that's who you've been taking up with! I should have known you would pick up with the trashiest boy in the county," she screamed as Jeopardy managed to crawl away and didn't waste any time getting to her feet. Loxley began to cry, and Addison clutched her stomach.

I stood between the two of them but kept my head down, in case Momma decided to rain down her fury on me. "Run, Jeopardy!" I whispered, and she ran up the stairs.

Momma didn't slap me, but she twisted my arm and warned, "You mind your own business, Harper Louise!"

"Momma, please!" I squealed as I twisted away. It was alright, though. Jeopardy had escaped, and I heard the door slam behind her. Momma headed up the stairs after her, but not before she grabbed her brush with the red handle from the parlor side table.

Loxley cried furiously now, and I squatted in front of her. "You and Addison go outside. Go to the potting shed. I'll come find you. Okay?"

She poked out her bottom lip. "Is this like Hide and Seek?"

"Exactly like Hide and Seek, but you might have to count to a hundred before I come, okay?"

"Okay, Harper."

"Take care of her, Addie." Addison nodded and wiped her tears away as the two of them went out the back door and into the yard. I wouldn't be able to stop Momma from beating Jeopardy, but maybe my presence would deter her, at least a little. I really didn't know what I would do except try to stop the inevitable, horrible ending.

I prayed as I bolted up the stairs, "Please, God, don't let Momma hurt Jeopardy. Daddy, if you're here, help us. Send a whole army of angels to help us." I moved quickly across the first landing and then on to the next flight of stairs. Momma banged on Jeopardy's castle door with her hairbrush, they shouted swear words at one another, and all I could do was cry. I stepped into the hallway and nearly fell backward.

A lady all in white swooshed in front of me, passing from one door to the one across the hallway. I could hardly believe my eyes. There were only six rooms up here, and two of them were closets, but she was moving between them. Her face twisted, and her dark hair flowed behind her. She appeared to be a young woman in a white dress with a faded gray rose between her breasts. Her hair hung down her back in ringlets, and her hands were clutching her stomach. I froze. There she was again!

She passed from one closet to another and then slid straight down the hallway toward Momma, who was standing at the top of the attic staircase. My mother didn't notice the woman in white. She rammed her left shoulder against the door, striking it repeatedly and obviously hoping to knock it down.

"Open this door, Jeopardy! You open it now!"

"No! Go away! I hate you! You killed Daddy, and now you want to kill me!"

I watched in horror as the woman sailed on toward her target. Just at the last moment, Momma swung around with her brush. She must have thought it was me coming up behind her. Her face was a mask of terror as she swung through the invisible woman. She fell forward down the staircase in a heap with a terrified scream.

And then the woman was gone.

Chapter Sixteen—Harper

The days after Momma's fall were a blur. The ambulance came about a half hour after my call, and she remained unconscious until they arrived. I don't think she immediately remembered any of what happened, but she must have recalled the horrific moment by the time she got home with her face bruised and her arm broken. The Lady in White put the fear of God in Momma. She never spanked any of us again after that, and Jeopardy, who knew nothing about that ghost (or so I then believed), enjoyed new freedom. And so did I.

Aunt Dot moved in for a while to help take care of her sister and largely left us to entertain ourselves. School would start soon, and for the first time ever we had new clothes to wear, thanks entirely to her. These weren't just church hand-me-downs either. Aunt Dot bought me two sweaters, one pink and one blue, matching skirts and two pale yellow shirts. I loved every item, as did we all. Even Jeopardy got new clothes, and I saw her hug our aunt more than once.

"Come on, Harper. Let's go," Jeopardy said when she appeared in my doorway one day. She usually spent all her time in her castle whenever she was home, but since Momma was incapacitated, my sister visited my room too. Loxley spent a lot of time on the second floor; she claimed to be playing with Daddy, and I didn't doubt her. Summerleigh had become a house of spirits. I ventured upstairs once after Momma's accident in search of the lady. There was no trace of the ghost, except I thought I saw the trailing edge of her skirt as it slipped away into a closet. That could have been my own imagination, but it was enough for me. I pried Jeopardy for information about the ghost to no avail.

"Where are we going?"

"To the river. I want to swim."

I flipped the pages of my magazine and pretended to be bored by her offer. Loxley and Addison were attending a birthday party today. Connie Loper had picked them up about an hour ago, so there wasn't much to do. I didn't have to do all the chores like before; Aunt Dot did most of them now. I wondered how long that would last. "I don't have a bathing suit."

"You don't need one. Come on, Harper Louise. Stop being such a stick in the mud."

"You two come back before dark, please." Aunt Dot paused in the doorway with a basket of folded laundry in her arms. "Or thereabouts. Augustine Hogue is coming over tonight to visit your mother, and I thought that would be a great time for us to go get some ice cream."

"Okay, Aunt Dot," Jeopardy agreed with a wrinkled nose and waved at me to come on.

Aunt Dot rolled her eyes at the sound of Momma yelling her name. "Coming, Ann. Patience, my dear."

I slid on my tennis shoes, grabbed a towel and followed Jeopardy to the back door of Summerleigh. I had never experienced liberty like this! It was dreamlike and somehow felt dangerous—and I never wanted it to end. For a split second, I saw a face on the top floor in the window closest to Jeopardy's castle room.

Daddy!

That was no woman but clearly a man—a man in uniform. Could it be Daddy?

"Did you see that?"

"Let's go, Harper. Stop dawdling." Jeopardy grabbed my hand and dragged me away without listening to a word I said.

"I swear I saw Daddy. And the night Momma fell...you have to know the truth! She didn't really fall, Jeopardy. The Lady in White pushed her down those stairs. Well, Momma took a swing at her and then fell. It all happened so fast, but the ghost was definitely there. I think she was trying to help you."

"Too little, too late," she muttered. "No more talk about ghosts, Harper. You shouldn't be afraid of ghosts. It's the living you have to worry about."

"I'm not afraid of Daddy if that was him. But the other one...she could have killed Momma."

Jeopardy stopped to light a cigarette and frowned. "She didn't. No more ghost stories. Let's run the rest of the way."

"You can't run and smoke, Jeopardy," I said with a grin.

"Come on, pie-face. I can outrun you with two cigarettes in my mouth." She took off, and I chased her with a faux growl.

"You know I hate that nickname!" We laughed all the way to the river. With every pump of my legs, I felt the weight of the past horrible months melt away. For once in my life, I was going to be a girl my age. Whatever that meant.

There were more kids at the river than I had ever seen before, at least twenty teenagers. Some were smoking, and most were swimming. Jeopardy sauntered up like she owned the place, her wild hair tumbling down her back. Why she didn't bob her hair, I would never know, but the wildness suited her. My sister was the most beautiful girl in the world, and the saddest.

Except for now, except for this moment. The Harvester boys were there, all three of them. The oldest, Tony, strolled over and kissed her cheek. She kissed him back and took the soda he offered her. He had a nice car with a swanky radio that played Count Basie's *I Want a Little Girl*. How strange that we would hear that song today. Daddy used to dance with us girls every Christmas. At our last Christmas together, this had been our song. I suddenly had the urge to run back to Summerleigh, back to Daddy.

"Jeopardy, we should go home." I touched her elbow, but she cast me that look that said, *Get lost.*

One of the girls from school, Arnette Loper, walked over. "Hey, Harper. You'll be in the ninth grade this year, right? Me too. Maybe we'll get the same teacher. I hope we get Mr. Dempsey. He's dreamy." Another girl, I couldn't remember her name, giggled.

"Mr. Dempsey? Is he the one with the sad eyes?" I asked as I glanced at Jeopardy, who was guzzling her drink.

Arnette giggled and took my hand. "Yes, and boy, howdy. I wish he'd make those sad eyes at me. You want to go swim?"

I looked at Jeopardy again. Seeing as she wasn't in a big hurry to hang out with me, I said, "Sure."

"Come on, then. It must be so neat having Jeopardy Belle for a sister. Did she really kiss Tony Harvester after church last spring?"

"I don't think so," I said honestly. "First I've heard of it."

"Good, because he's going to be mine one day. Unless you like him," she added suspiciously.

"Uh, no thanks. I think I'll hold out for Mr. Dempsey."

We traveled down the hill to the river and eased into the warm water. Arnette carried on with her gossiping, and I agreed with her on most points as we splashed. I wasn't in the water five minutes before Jeopardy came down. To my complete surprise, she stripped off her shirt and shorts and dived into the dark blue-brown water wearing only her underwear. Every eye was on her, including Troy Harvester's. He was pouting, his arms crossed, staring at her with his big blue eyes like a hound dog that'd been banned from the porch. I knew he still loved her, or something, even after Momma's bad behavior.

Jeopardy didn't come up from the water right away. Just when I began to worry, she reappeared a good ten feet away, rising out of the water like a siren. Her face was turned toward the sun, and her hands were above her head. She swam toward me. "Hey, pie-face." She kissed my cheek and dived under again. I forgot all about frog-faced Arnette and played with my sister. We ducked and dived, trying to grab each other. This was the most fun I'd had with Jeopardy since we were just small kids.

And then Troy was there.

He'd shed his shirt but still wore his blue jean shorts, thank goodness. If any of these boys took off their clothing, I'd have to go home. I wasn't prepared to see a naked boy.

Jeopardy bobbed back up and splashed back in surprise when she noticed him. The three of us were alone now, since Arnette and her blond friend were trolling the other two Harvester boys. I felt like a third wheel, but I wasn't about to leave Jeopardy alone swimming around in her underwear. The two of them faced one another; Jeopardy's tan face glistened in the setting sun, and Troy's blond hair poked up as it quickly dried in the heat. It looked like cotton.

"I want to know something, Jeopardy Belle."

"What's that, Troy Harvester?"

"Why don't you ever kiss me? You kissed my brother just now. Right in front of me. I thought you liked me, but you don't kiss me. Why is that? I know your Momma hates me. I heard her call me trash."

She backed away from him but didn't go too far. She tilted her head and watched him as she continued to tread water. Her hazel eyes were hard and full of hurt. "I don't kiss you because I like you, Troy. And I don't care what my Momma says."

He wiped the water from his face and kept treading water. "Then stop kissing everyone else."

"You don't know a dang thing, Troy Harvester. Why don't you go find someone else to kiss on? Come on, Harper. It's time to go."

She was angry now. She splashed out of the water, ignoring the stares as she got dressed, and together we left the party. I guessed that was a party. I didn't have any punch, but it felt like a party. Kind of.

As we walked, her mood darkened. She smoked, and I walked beside her. I had to ask her the same question. "Why don't you kiss Troy, Jep? Is he gross or something? Got stank breath?"

"No, it's nothing like that."

"Then why?" I laughed as I tried to smooth my drying hair with my hands.

"Because Troy Harvester deserves a better girl than me."

I didn't know how to answer that. We didn't talk the rest of the way home.

Chapter Seventeen—Jerica

When I got out of bed Sunday, I felt like a truck had run over me. My sheets were sweaty, and my teeth and skin felt filmy. The reflection in the mirror didn't do much to boost my morale. At least I felt somewhat normal now. Moving slowly, my sore back muscles screaming, I stepped into the shower and washed away the remnants of whatever germ had held me prisoner for the past few days. During those feverish days and nights, I had dreamed.

The Lady in White had pushed Ann down the stairs! Was she protecting Jeopardy, or was she merely a spirit bent on bringing harm to anyone who crossed her path? Was this Mariana McIntyre?

And then I remembered Jeopardy's notes, the ones she crammed into walls and floorboards. Harper had never found them, but I had to. My stomach growling, I stepped out of the steamy shower feeling almost human again. I kept things casual with shorts and a tank top. I was so hungry, I could eat a bear, as my friend Anita used to say. Where was a good bear when you needed one?

Nothing in my refrigerator appealed to me, so I settled on a few fried eggs and some toast. But before I could get the skillet out, I heard a knock at the front door. It was Jesse's cousin, Renee.

"Hey, Jerica. I hope you don't mind me coming by, but I was in the neighborhood with a casserole..." She grinned at me.

"I don't mind at all, and perfect timing. I hate cooking for myself. Not to mention I'm not too good at it."

"Great, lead me to the kitchen."

"I'm glad you didn't come by yesterday. I've been a bit under the weather."

"I figured it must be something. I thought for sure you'd come hear Jesse play."

"Why would you think that 'for sure'?"

"I don't know. Just a feeling, but honestly, you didn't miss anything," she said as she pulled a plate out of the cabinet and served a slice of what looked to be a chicken casserole.

"Poor turnout?" I asked as I offered her a glass of tea.

"None for me, thanks. No, we had a great turnout. Poor playing. Jesse is a lot of things, a talented carpenter, even a good short-order cook...but a guitar player, he is not."

I laughed to hear that. "Oh no. I'm glad I stayed home then."

"Feeling better today?"

"Sure am. And luckily, I'm a nurse."

"Well, if you ever need a good doctor, go see Dr. Leland. He's the best doctor in George County, as far as I'm concerned."

"Leland?" That got my attention. This had to be a relative of Jeopardy's peach-loving doctor.

"Yeah, he's with that group in town. Nice guy. He went to school with my older sister, Rebecca. I think he had a thing for her, but nothing ever happened between them. So, what are your plans for today?"

The casserole was delicious, so much so I was tempted to ask for the recipe...but who was I kidding? I probably wasn't going to ever cook such a dish. "I'm probably going to explore Summerleigh. May I ask you a question?"

"Sure. I'm an open book."

"What scared you the other day?"

She shook her head. "That's really one of the reasons I came by, I had to tell you the truth. Someone shoved me. I felt a hand in the middle of my back, forcing me out of the master bedroom. I got the distinct impression that it was Ann Belle. She doesn't like you being here, or me, for that matter."

"I can totally see that being the case. She was not a nice lady. How in the world did she ever land a guy like John?"

"There are rumors about Ann; she was rough on those girls. But at one time she was the loveliest lady in George County. She even represented the state as Miss Mississippi, but her pageant days were cut short. In those days, unmarried and pregnant disqualified you from a lot of things."

"Wait, what?"

"Yep. That's the rumor, and Jesse verified it with his research. Either Jeopardy Belle was born three months early or something else happened."

"Oh, that explains a lot. She must have really resented Jeopardy." I sipped my tea and then asked, "What about John? Did he ever raise any questions about his oldest daughter?"

"He never did. John Jeffrey Belle is a town hero, even though he didn't die in the war. Before the accident he earned many awards, including one for bravery, what do they call it? I can't remember, but he was such a beautiful man. Did you know they have a statue of him right off Main Street?"

"No, but I don't know much about the area. Virginia seems a long way away now."

"You'll do fine. Want some more?" She gestured toward the casserole.

"No, I'm stuffed. Did JB win the house from a McIntyre? What do you know about Mariana McIntyre?"

"JB? You mean John Belle? No, I don't think he won Summerleigh from a McIntyre. They all died out at the turn of the last century. However, it can't be hard to figure out who owned the house before the Belles. It stood empty a lot of years before John claimed it. Jesse probably knows, but darned if I can remember. As far as Mariana goes, John became kind of obsessed with the family history. When he wasn't fixing up the place, he was at the library digging up information."

"Information about what?"

"Girl, that was before my time."

"Way before your time, of course. Want to walk with me? I'd like to check out something in the attic at Summerleigh, and honestly, I'd feel better if I had someone with me. Would you think I was crazy if I told you that I've seen Ann?"

"Nope. Not crazy at all. And I don't blame you. Just from my short survey the other day, I knew there were spirits lingering around. Summerleigh has never been a happy place." I couldn't hide my worried expression. "Oh, I mean until now. You'll make it a wonderful place. I'm sure of it."

"What else did you see the other day? Anything?"

"No, that was it. I didn't see a thing, but I felt that hand as sure as I'm sitting here. The touch of those cold fingers freaked me out. I mean, I knew the place was spiritually active. It had to be; it's so old and all, and so much tragedy has happened here, but I wasn't prepared for that."

"Do you think Jeopardy Belle is in that house? I'm only asking because I made Harper a promise. I promised I would find her sister, and I've been having these..." My face flushed. Imagine telling a near stranger that I'd been dreaming about Harper as a girl, about ghosts, and that I'd seen my dead daughter here at Summerleigh.

"Go on, Jerica. You can tell me. What have you seen? Have you seen a girl?"

"I've seen a lot of things but not Jeopardy's ghost. I'm not sure she's here, but I have to find out. I know this sounds strange, but I think she left clues. Notes in the walls and floorboards of the attic."

"What makes you think that?"

I bit my lip and then took a sip of my tea. "Because Harper told me." I got up to put my plate in the sink when a wave of dizziness came over me. "Whoa," I said as I waited out the spiraling scene.

"Hey, you better sit down. I don't think you're up to a field trip today. In fact, I'm not sure it's a good idea for you to go back into Summerleigh alone. Not in your current state. They say negative entities tend to latch on when we're physically weak. I know for a fact there is at least one negative spirit in that house."

"How do you know so much about this stuff?" I asked as she took the plate from my hand and helped me back to my seat.

"I grew up seeing spirits, hearing voices. My family all thought I was crazy until my uncle came back from the grave and told me where he'd left his truck keys. Nobody's given me any crap since then."

"Really? That happened to you?"

"Yeah, but it was a long time ago. Nothing as amazing has happened since, but I still see and feel things from time to time."

"And Jesse?"

"Ha! No way would he admit it, but I have my suspicions." I laughed to hear about it. "May I suggest something?"

"Sure."

"I have a friend, Hannah Ray. She's the best psychic medium I know. Why not let her walk Summerleigh with us? She might be able to tell us who is in there and who's not."

"I don't know, Renee. No offense to you or your friend, but I've never believed in any of that stuff."

"I'm not offended, but I am surprised. How can you not believe in what you've seen yourself? And you have someone with you all the time. A child, I think. I can only see her outline, but she's always near you. And from time to time, she touches you. I've seen you turn your head in her direction when she's close. Is she a relative?"

I burst into tears, and when I could stop crying I told Renee the complete story. By the time she'd left, she'd called Hannah and made an appointment for tomorrow.

"If anyone can contact Marisol, it is Hannah. I am sorry for your loss, Jerica, but I am glad you are here. Why don't you try to get some rest?"

"I think I will. Let me walk you to the door first, though."

"No need, I can find my way out. I'll see you tomorrow at eleven."

"Bye, Renee." I heard the door close and crawled onto my wicker couch to sleep. I didn't have long to wait.

Chapter Eighteen—Harper

A month later, Aunt Dot still hadn't left us despite Momma's increasingly obnoxious behavior. For all her ugly ways, I felt sorry for Momma and spent time with her a little while every day now that she could move around. Weeks had gone by before we had been allowed in her room; I think she didn't want us to see her with those bruises on her face. But I had great news today, and as she had made it all the way to the parlor, I had to tell her. Maybe she would be proud of me.

"Momma, guess what? I got voted into the Harvest Queen Court. Isn't that wonderful?" I asked nervously as I held her hand.

"You did? I am delighted to hear that. I knew you could do it, Harper. Of all my girls, you are certainly the smartest." I noticed she didn't say loveliest, but if smartest was all I could get, I would happily receive it. "Tell me all about the competition. Were there many girls vying for a court spot? That horrible Loper girl, the one with the frog face, is she in this court?"

"No, ma'am. She didn't make the cut." I didn't mean that in a mean way, but Momma thought it was hilarious. She laughed and gossiped about Arnette's mother for a few minutes. I smiled politely even though my subconscious warned me that by befriending Momma I was betraying Jeopardy; I knew it, but I could not help myself. I craved Momma's approval more than anything in the world. Except maybe Jeopardy's friendship. How unfortunate that those two things were in direct contrast to one another. After I provided my mother with all the details, she excitedly instructed me to pick a gown from her closet. I would need a nice one.

Aunt Dot joined our merry conversation, and between the three of us, we found a dress that would be suitable for such an important event. Of course, it was a formal gown and for the life of me, I had no recollection of Momma having ever worn such a beautiful, heavenly gown. It was light blue with shimmering rhinestones all over it.

"A fairy princess!" My aunt clapped her hands in approval.

"Oh, but her shoes, Dorothy. We will never get those size nines into my size sevens. Never ever, and without the right shoes, she will be a laughingstock." Was Momma changing her mind? Would she take the magical gown back?

Aunt Dot chewed her lip. "I know where to find the perfect shoes. I saw them in a store on Main Street. We'll go pick up a pair this afternoon, Harper. Why don't you come with us, Ann? It would be good to see you get out of the house for a while."

"No, I think I'll try to wash my hair; it's an absolute mess. But you girls have fun." Momma left my room and went into her own, closing the door behind her. I hated that our pleasant time had ended, but at least she had lent me her gown. Aunt Dot and I chatted about jewelry, but a knock at the front door put a pause in our conversation.

Aunt Dot opened the door, and my heart sank when I saw our visitor. It was Deputy Lonnie Passeau. He swung his key ring on his finger and gazed down at Aunt Dot as if she were a bug he'd like to squash. Or something. I'd seen him around the school a few times; apparently, some boys had spray-painted the outside of the gym and had gotten expelled for it. And now he was here. That couldn't be good.

It could only mean one thing. Jeopardy was in trouble.

"Good afternoon, Deputy. How may I help you?"

"Well, good afternoon, Miss Daughdrill. May I come in a moment?"

"Actually," Aunt Dot said as she stepped out on the porch and closed the door behind her, "my sister isn't really up to visitors right now. Is there something I might help you with?"

"Maybe so, maybe so," he said as he flipped his key ring around. "The sheriff is really interested in cleaning up the riffraff that tends to congregate around the river on the weekends. Those kids go down there drinking, smoking and doing God knows what, and it has to stop before someone gets hurt...or otherwise damaged. Now, I don't consider any daughter of John Jeffrey Belle's to be riffraff—the man was a war hero—but his oldest girl, Jeopardy, she's been participating in some shocking behavior as of late. I thought it best to tell her mother, in hopes that she could encourage Jeopardy to behave in a more ladylike fashion."

"No, sir. I can't believe my niece would do anything like that." Aunt Dot was lying; she knew Jeopardy smoked and had even tried to discourage her a few times to no avail. Jep would do what she wanted to do, no matter who said anything to her. "And as far as the river goes, it's a public swimming hole, isn't it?"

Passeau answered in his deep voice. He was clearly losing patience with Aunt Dot. "Perhaps you aren't the one I should be speaking with after all. Since you don't have any children of your own, you may not understand how crucial it is to be a good example to a child. When would be a good time for me to speak to Ann, I mean, Mrs. Belle?"

Aunt Dot's voice shook. "I couldn't say. I will tell my sister you stopped by when she wakes up from her nap. I am sure she will call you if she has any questions."

"I need to have a word with Jeopardy," he said as he shoved his keys into his pocket and tucked his hat down over his eye. I think he spotted me behind the lace curtain, and I ducked down to avoid further detection.

"No, I think that can wait. I'll speak to Jeopardy, Deputy."

He nodded and stepped down off the porch. "I'll hold you to that, Miss Daughdrill. If I find her misbehaving at the river, she will have to spend some time in the back of my squad car. Good afternoon now." With a grin, he walked back to his car, and

Aunt Dot came inside looking like she'd lost all the blood in her face.

With her back against the door, she said, "Harper, warn your sister to stay away from that man." And that was all she said. She went into the kitchen and called someone on the phone, but I couldn't hear her muffled conversation.

Just then, Loxley tugged on my hand. "I found a treasure, Harper. A real-life treasure. You want to see it?" Her eyes were gleeful, and she was jumping up and down with excitement.

"I hope you haven't been plundering Momma's jewelry boxes, Loxley."

"No, these treasures belong to the lady upstairs. You want to see them?"

I swallowed at the mention of the Lady in White; that had to be who Loxley was speaking about. I glanced at the doorway, but Aunt Dot was still on the phone. "Yes, show me." We made our way up to the top floor, and Loxley opened the door of the attic. "Jeopardy won't like us being in her castle, Loxley. We should go now."

"Oh no, I haven't gotten into any of her things, not even her notes. Did you know she leaves notes for the ghosts?"

"Does she?" I had seen her once depositing a note but had been unable to retrieve it. "Have you read any of them?"

"You know I can't read." She frowned at me as if I were stupid. "The treasure box is over here, Harper, but you cannot tell anyone that I showed it to you. Not even Jeopardy. She doesn't come to this side of the attic."

"Okay, mum's the word."

We tiptoed through the many boxes and strange finds until we came to an old trunk. *It must be old*, I thought. I studied the lock and saw the numbers *1870* and some letters engraved near the opening. The letters were scratched, so I couldn't tell what they were. Two M's, maybe? "Is it locked?"

"No, it's open. I found this treasure; does that mean it's mine?"

"I don't know, Loxley. It must belong to someone. What's inside?"

We opened the trunk, and I was amazed at the contents. A ruffled pink gown caught my attention first. We carefully removed it, and I immediately held it up to myself and asked, "What do you think?"

"It's my treasure, Harper." She poked her bottom lip out at me, and I put the dress to the side.

"Alright, if it doesn't belong to anyone else, it is your treasure."

"Do ghosts own treasures?"

"I'm not sure. Why?"

She dug around in the trunk, obviously looking for something. "She wears that dress sometimes. Only it's all white when she wears it."

I spun around and stared at the dress. She was right! The Lady in White had worn that dress the night I saw her on the stairs, when she scared Momma nearly to death. "Oh, Loxley. I think you need to put this back. This isn't our treasure. It's hers."

"But she won't mind. She likes me; she smiles at me all the time. And look at this." She held a tiny snow globe in her hands. Shaking it up, she held her palm out so I could watch the snow fall.

"Let me see," I said, ignoring her pout. She didn't want to part with any of this stuff, but I could tell she had laid claim to this prize. I held the snow globe up to the light. The water was slightly cloudy...how old could this be? In the center of the "snow" storm stood two tiny figures, a man and a woman. They were dressed for an old-fashioned Christmas. The man wore a plaid coat, and the lady a plaid hat. Their mouths were open in perpetual song, probably a Christmas carol judging by the tiny hymnbook they held.

I could hardly believe it, but the man in the plaid coat looked exactly like Daddy. Daddy and the Lady in White were standing in the snow together singing their silent song! The room became cold, and I had never wanted to leave a place more than I did right now. "We have to go, Loxley. We have to go now." I tossed the dress back in the trunk and snatched the globe away from her and placed it back inside the trunk.

"No, Harper! That's my treasure. It's okay that I have it. She doesn't mind!"

I took her hand and ignored her complaint. To my horror, the attic door was closing. Even Loxley gasped.

"It's just the wind, Harper. It does that sometimes. It's just the wind, right?" Her whispering gave my goose bumps goose bumps.

"Hush," I warned as we tiptoed to the door. I put my hand on the doorknob and slowly began to turn it.

And then we heard the floorboard outside the door squeaking. Someone was out there. I let go of the doorknob and watched in terror as it began to shake, as if someone wanted to get in. We stepped back a few steps, Loxley's little arms went around my waist and she closed her eyes.

"Make him go away, Harper. Make the boy go away."

I held on to her and closed my eyes. The shaking stopped, and we collapsed on Jeopardy's pallet, waiting until we felt safe to leave. We didn't have long to wait; the door opened about five minutes later, and Jeopardy yelled at us.

"Don't come in my castle when I'm not here. What are you doing? Snooping through my things?" She cut her eyes to a plain wooden box in the corner near her pillow, but we both shook our heads.

"No! Loxley found a treasure, over there, but I told her to put it back. And then when we tried to leave, the door started shaking and we couldn't get out. We didn't touch a thing! I swear!"

"Swear!" Loxley repeated, raising her hand as if she were ready to pledge on a stack of Bibles.

"Fine, but don't come back up here without my permission. I have traps in place, and you'll get hurt."

"Fine," I said, aggravated at her lack of compassion. Didn't she realize a ghost could have gotten us? Loxley took off out of the room, but I lingered a moment.

"Deputy Passeau came by today looking for you. He says you've been behaving badly down at the river. He's going to arrest you, Jeopardy Belle, if he catches you doing bad again."

"Is he?" She struck a match and smoked a thin cigarette. Likely one of Momma's. "Did he tell Momma?" She smiled gleefully.

"No, he told Aunt Dot, and she wasn't happy about it."

"I wish he would have told Momma. That would have been better. I wish he would have told her. I would have loved to have seen her face."

"Why do you do this, Jeopardy? Why do you always have to make trouble? Why do you hate Momma so much? Why can't you let sleeping dogs lie?"

"Get out of my castle, pie-face! And don't come back." She got in my face and poked my chest with her finger. I was a full foot taller than her, but it didn't matter. She was stronger; she was always stronger than me. "If you side with my enemy, then you're my enemy too, Harper."

"I have never been your enemy, Jeopardy," I said as my heart broke and the tears came unbidden. "Please go to Momma. Tell her you're sorry. We can be a family again. Daddy would want us to love each other."

"Get out!" she screamed angrily.

And I did, suddenly unafraid of any ghost or spirit. The only thing I had been afraid of, losing my sister's friendship, had happened. I had crossed the line, and she would never forgive me.

Never ever.

Chapter Nineteen—Harper

Aunt Dot left a trail of sad faces behind this morning. I think all of us Belle girls had halfway hoped that she'd make the change of address permanent, but it wasn't to be. In the end, Aunt Dot looked tired, too tired to continue caring for Momma, who had obviously decided at some point that she didn't need her sister's help anymore. She'd dressed and decided to go to the ladies' auxiliary meeting at the church. Augustine Hogue would be there too, and thankfully, I wasn't asked to accompany them. Jeopardy had come home early this morning silly-giddy. I suspected she had been drinking, but I didn't ask her. I don't think our other sisters noticed.

"Hey, I have an idea. Let's have a party," Jeopardy said with a giggle.

"Like a birthday party?" Loxley asked expectantly. "Whose birthday is it?"

"Nobody's birthday, silly goose. It's just a party. You can have a party for no reason at all if you like. Let's turn on the radio and dance."

Addison coughed up a storm but didn't object. When she finished hacking, she said in her perpetually squeaky voice, "We don't know any dances. Show us some of your dances, Jeopardy."

"Okay, but you have to be my partner, Addie. No, you have to try. Now stand like this." Loxley and I giggled as Jeopardy showed Addison how to properly hold her partner; her left arm around Jeopardy's waist, her right hand in hers. They looked like the top of a wedding cake, except with two girls, not a bride and groom. Even Addison laughed as they shuffled through the waltz. "It's hard to teach you when you won't stop laughing," Jeopardy complained good-naturedly.

"Teach Harper, Jeopardy. She's going to be the Harvest Queen at school." Loxley clapped and then strutted around the room waving as if she'd won the award herself.

"Really? First I heard of it."

"I'm not the queen, and it's no big deal," I said defensively while casting a warning eye at Loxley.

"Oh yes it *is* a big deal. You should see the dress Momma gave her to wear. It's blue with star sparkles all over it. She looks like Miss America." Loxley ignored my warning stare and offered more waving and an over-accentuated prissy walk. Addison roared at her antics.

"I don't walk like that, Loxley!"

"Who's taking you to this dance, Harper? Not one of those Harvester boys, I hope."

I shook my head. I knew who she was talking about. How could she think I would go to a dance with Troy Harvester? I alone knew how she felt about him. Our conversation from our walk home from the river rang in my head. "Nobody. I am going solo, Jeopardy. Is that so bad?"

"Yes, that's terrible," she said with her hand cocked on her hip. "Don't y'all think that's terrible?" Our sisters agreed with Jeopardy.

Loxley quickly added, "Maybe you could invite Ray Loper from church? I am sure he'd look fine in a suit."

"Yuck. No thank you."

"Loxley's right. You should tell Ray to take you. He would. I know he would. I'll talk to him if you like," Jeopardy said with a cryptic smile.

"Can we talk about something else? I don't want to go to the dance with anyone."

Jeopardy's smile disappeared. "Liar, liar, pants on fire. Let me teach you some moves, Harper, so you don't embarrass us all."

"Fine," I said as I surrendered to Jeopardy's tutelage. We must have lost track of time because before we knew it, Momma's car was pulling in the driveway. I thought maybe Jeopardy would run upstairs since she hardly spent any time in Momma's presence anymore, but she didn't. She walked in behind us with her arms crossed.

"You girls hungry? My, you all look so pink-cheeked. What have you been doing?" Momma unpacked a casserole and took the tea pitcher out of the refrigerator.

"Dancing! Jeopardy has been teaching us." As always, Loxley volunteered too much information. She couldn't help it, I knew that, but I wished she'd shut up from time to time.

"Just the waltz," I added. "Can I help you with something, Momma?"

"Get the plates, Harper. Why don't you collect the silverware, Jeopardy? Addison can pour the drinks."

We all set about our tasks; even Loxley folded napkins. For one moment, I pretended we were a normal family; I enjoyed the feeling, but those moments never lasted very long. Actually, they were quite dangerous. They lulled you into believing that all was well. It never was. Not at our house.

Momma put the dish on the table, along with some bread. I knew right away Jeopardy wasn't going to touch it. It was spaghetti with stewed tomatoes. If there was anything Jeopardy hated, it was a stewed tomato. Raw ones off the vine or sliced with salt and pepper were okay, but not slimy, stewed ones. She'd gotten sick on them years ago and never forgot that sickness. Even today they made her gag. Still, Momma slopped a big old pile of the pasta and tomatoes on Jeopardy's plate and plunked it down in front of her. Jeopardy flashed her an *I-hate-you* look and then sat back in the cane chair with her arms still crossed.

"Harper, you say grace, dear." Momma bowed her perfect, pretty head and folded her hands. Everyone followed suit, except Jeopardy, who continued to bore holes into the top of our mother's head.

"Dear Lord, bless our food. Make it nourish our bodies, in Jesus' name. Amen."

Whenever asked to say grace, which wasn't often, I always used Daddy's prayer. I couldn't help but think about Daddy now. He loved to slurp his spaghetti noodles. He didn't cut up his pasta and eat it politely. Spaghetti nights at our house had been fun, once upon a time. And completely free of stewed tomatoes. Jeopardy ate the bread and then started to get up when Momma put her fork down.

"Where do you think you're going? I haven't excused you yet. There's been far too much laxity of decorum around here while I've been down with my arm. Aunt Dorothy must have let you all run wild. Have you forgotten your manners completely, Jeopardy Harris Belle?"

Jeopardy didn't speak but wiped her face with her napkin. She wasn't shaking in her boots, not like me. Addison was drinking her tea and looking green. Loxley alone enjoyed her feast, but even she ate with wide eyes as we watched the expected argument unfold.

"I asked you a question, Jeopardy. Have you forgotten your manners?"

Jeopardy banged her fist on the table. "Yes, I have. Do you want me to tell everyone when I lost my *manners*, Momma? Would you like the details? All those details? Maybe I should tell my sisters all about it too." She banged the table with both fists now and stood up threateningly.

Momma leaned back, surprised at her oldest daughter's outburst. I didn't know why she would be surprised, but she sure acted like it.

"Don't speak to me in that tone, girl! Do you all hear how disrespectful she is to your poor mother? All I tried to do was bring a nice dinner home from the church, and this is my thanks." Nobody answered. The three of us, Addison, Loxley and I, kept our eyes on our plates as Jeopardy huffed in frustration at us—no, at me. What did she want from me? I couldn't help her. What could I say that would help? Momma wouldn't beat Jeopardy anymore, not since her accident, not since she saw that ghost, but she would certainly beat me. And I had a dance to go to. In that moment, I realized the horrible truth. I was tee-totally selfish, as selfish as selfish could be.

"Harper?" Jeopardy whispered hopefully, but I wouldn't look up. All my promises to stick with her, to stay by her side, disappeared like fog on the water. The only sound you could hear in our kitchen was the sound of Momma's chewing. She carried on with her dinner like Jeopardy was a rude stranger she hoped to ignore.

"Addison, please pass me the parmesan, dear." With shaking hands, Addie obeyed and the rest of us sat and waited for the storm to either pass or explode.

With a sob of betrayal, Jeopardy left the kitchen. I heard her footsteps running up the stairs to her castle. Momma acted like she didn't hear a thing. She dabbed the corners of her mouth with her napkin and smiled at Loxley. "Eat up like a big girl."

"Yes, ma'am." Loxley toyed with her food and cast a convicting glance in my direction. I couldn't stand it. I had to go see about Jeopardy. We'd gotten so close over the past few weeks, and I'd let her down. What if she hurt herself? I couldn't have that on my conscience.

"Momma, may I be..." Before I could finish my sentence, the radio in the parlor came on at full volume. It was Count Basie, playing *I Want a Little Girl*. Momma ran to the parlor to scold Jeopardy for playing with her radio, but she wasn't there. Nobody was there. Jeopardy had gone upstairs anyway. How could she be in two places at one time?

The room was empty, and the air was icy cold.

Loxley stiffened beside me. Momma was talking to herself, accusing us of playing with the radio when she knew with her own eyes that was impossible. We were all here, in the parlor with her. And we had all been in the kitchen with her before that.

"Daddy's here, Daddy and that lady. Something bad is going to happen," Loxley shouted. Then she began to cry.

Momma lost her temper. "Shut up with that caterwauling, Loxley! You girls go to bed. I've seen enough of your faces today. Go on now." Momma stood with her hands on her hips, her face filled with fear and confusion, and we did as we were told. I stayed with my younger sisters that night. Something was going on here, things were happening that I couldn't see or understand, and no amount of persuasion would convince Loxley to stop crying and tell me. It didn't matter. I had a duty to protect my sisters from whatever bad thing Daddy was trying to warn us about, for surely that was why he was here. He watched over us still, but he would need my help.

Oh, Daddy! Why can't I see you? Help us! Help us all!

And later, when everyone was asleep, I would go upstairs to see Jeopardy. I had to tell her that I loved her.

That I was sorry for abandoning her, for being afraid, for not taking her side.

I stayed up for hours, waiting for Momma to go to bed. It was hard to pretend you were asleep when someone was watching you. Momma watched me for a full minute, even whispered my name, but I ignored her and hoped she wouldn't drag me out of the bed as she sometimes did. She didn't. God had at least heard my prayers tonight. Later, when the house got quiet, I crawled out of the bed and crept up the stairs, praying again for protection. *Please, God, keep the ghosts away unless it's Daddy.*

When I got to Jeopardy's door, I found it slightly ajar. I pushed it open, but she wasn't there. My heart dropped as I walked to her open window. The air smelled like dirt and rain. Yes, it would certainly rain tonight, and it would be here soon. One thing you could be sure of around here were evening storms. It would be that way until fall truly arrived, and then it would be dry and windy.

I opened my eyes just in time to see my sister running through the backyard. And she wasn't alone. A boy ran beside her, but who? I wanted to yell her name, but the risk was too great. What would happen if Momma knew Jeopardy had been off with a boy?

I shuddered at the thought. I heard footsteps in the hallway and became afraid that I wasn't alone. What if the door-slamming ghost showed up again? I tiptoed out of the room and back downstairs.

There was nothing I could do about Jeopardy tonight, but maybe tomorrow. Yes, tomorrow I would call Aunt Dot. I would tell her that horrible things were happening here and how much we missed her. She would know what to do. Someone had to help us with Momma.

I walked into my room and found my borrowed dress removed from the closet and spread out on the bed. The beautiful dress Momma had lent me was torn to shreds like someone had taken a knife to it. No, scissors. A big old pair of silver-plated scissors were lying beside the destroyed garment. I'd never seen those scissors before. Who would do such a thing? Jeopardy? Momma?

What would I wear to the Harvest Dance now?

Jeopardy, how could you be so cruel? I didn't mean to let you down. I was coming to apologize. My teenage heart felt heavy, and I cried myself to sleep clutching the blue fragments. Nothing would ever be right again.

Chapter Twenty—Jerica

Strange to think that the first social event I had at Summerleigh would be a ghost hunt. I wasn't sure what else to call this...it certainly wasn't a séance or anything like that. I kind of felt silly about the whole thing now, but it was too late to change my mind. Hannah, Renee and Jesse were here, although Jesse remained outside with the roofer, who had come to give me an estimate on the east wing. I was kind of glad he'd stayed out there.

Despite my reservations, I greeted the ladies politely and welcomed them into the old place. Hannah's eyes grew big. "Wow, so this is Summerleigh. I can see why you'd want to fix this place up. What a grand old lady! What will you do with her when you get the job complete? Will this be your family home, or do you have something else in mind?"

"I'm not sure, honestly. I'm not much for planning too far ahead anymore."

Hannah was tall, taller than me, with large eyes and a thin figure. Simply dressed in a blue and white dress, she had an old-fashioned purse on her shoulder that she clutched like someone might steal it. Maybe it was her lucky talisman and comforted her. Maybe it held her lucky charms. I had no idea.

Hannah touched my arm sympathetically. "You made a promise to someone. Someone who lived here." I nodded in agreement. She let me go and walked around the Great Room, stopping at the corner near the fireplace. "She was young back then, but she was old when you knew her. I can see her. She's with us."

"Yes, that's right," I said as I glanced at Renee suspiciously. "Harper Belle was a friend of mine."

"I didn't tell her a thing. I swear," Renee whispered.

"Your friend is not the only one here, and I don't think she stays here all the time. She comes and goes, but there are others who never leave." Birds began chirping on the front porch; I had noticed a nest in the porch roof earlier. Their chirps created a strange echo through the empty house. Hannah walked toward me. "Would you mind if I walked by myself for a little while?"

"Are you sure you want to?" I asked her.

"I'll be okay. If you could stay here, that would help me focus on the other energies here at Summerleigh rather than the one that follows you."

"Follows me? You mean Harper."

"Oh no. This isn't Harper Belle. This has to be a relative of yours. She looks very much like you, especially her eyes. Maybe a sister or a...oh, dear. I'm sorry. She's your daughter. Mary? No, that's not it." Hannah closed her eyes and appeared to be listening. "Marisol, what a lovely name."

"Yes, she was...she is my daughter. Is she here? Can I talk to her?" I tried not to cry.

"We can certainly talk to her, but there are others here, Jerica. We will come back to Marisol." I couldn't hide my disappointment, and she held my hands briefly. "I know you are eager to communicate with her, but that's best not done in here. You don't want to attach her to this place. No, you don't want that. It's best to leave the communication with her for later, at your own home so she won't be confused about where to find you when she feels she wants to connect."

"Okay," I said breathlessly as I blinked back tears. Hannah touched my arm again and continued her survey of the room.

"Yes, there are too many others present," she said, but I had no idea what she meant. "I'm coming up now," she called up the stairs. "I'm not here to take anything or to harm you." She paused at the bottom of the staircase and waved at us to stay back. "I'll be back in a few minutes."

"No, I want to go, too. As the homeowner, I can't let you get hurt. I won't say a peep, but you have to let us come with you. I know I'm not supposed to say anything but what I know—I mean, I guess that's the rule—but there is a lady. She caused Ann Belle to fall. I wouldn't want anything to happen to you."

"Alright," Hannah said, "but ask Marisol to stay down here. You don't want her getting involved in this."

I shivered at her words like a rabbit ran over my grave. "Marisol? Honey? Stay down here, okay.

Don't come up the stairs. Listen to Mommy." I waited, unsure if she'd heard me or if she was even here. How would I know? What if Hannah was playing some cruel joke on me? Renee was friendly and all, but I didn't really know her. She might be the sort of person to arrange such a prank. A horrible, cruel prank.

"Okay, I feel her leaving. Let's go upstairs and see who's waiting for us." The three of us slowly climbed the squeaky staircase. "This used to be such a beautiful place," Hannah said absently as she ran her hand over the wooden railing. "There was another house here before this one. It was smaller but just as grand." As we reached the landing, Hannah glanced down. I thought I heard something, like the shuffling of papers downstairs. Maybe it was Jesse? I hadn't heard him come in, but he could have come in the back door.

Renee whispered to us, "Did you hear that? Sounded like scratching or something."

"Like papers shuffling," I said.

"Yes, like someone was flipping the pages of a magazine or a newspaper in a quiet room. Oh, I can see her. She's not a very nice lady. She doesn't like our being here. And she doesn't like you at all, Jerica. She knows why you're here. Oh yes, she's angry. I think she's following us. Let's go upstairs quickly. She doesn't like it up here, so she won't come up. The others are up here."

"How many ghosts are in this place, Hannah?" Renee asked excitedly.

"So far, the one downstairs, the lady who looks like Grace Kelly. She's so angry, so full of hate. She tries to keep others away, the ones who want to come here. She has a secret, many secrets, but there are more energies here. A man, a child—a boy, I think— and another lady." We were walking the hallway of the second floor now. "The boy has been here longer than any of them. He's strong, and he's...evil. He stays mostly in this room."

I recognized the room as Loxley's playroom. "How can a child be evil?" I asked.

"I don't know, but that's what I feel. He's disappointed because there are no kids to play with. Oh, God. Don't let kids in here, not until he's gone. He won't tell me his name. He wants to know where the girl is, the one he used to play with in here. They played these kinds of games..." Hannah closed her eyes and clapped her hands, and I couldn't help but think of Loxley.

"Hand-clapping games? He played with one of the Belle children, Loxley."

"He wanted Loxley to do something bad, and she wouldn't play with him anymore," Hannah said. "What is your name?" she asked the boy aloud. "Tell me your name."

I heard nothing, and Hannah frowned. Obviously, she didn't hear anything either. Apparently, this boy wasn't willing to share any information with her. Although sunlight filled the room, it felt clammy and unwelcoming in here. I hadn't noticed that before. A board squeaked near the window. *Must be the house warming up. Boards creak from time to time, Jerica.* I didn't want to be here anymore and wished I hadn't insisted on coming along.

"Stop that," Hannah warned him. "You can't hurt us." She frowned again and turned away from the window where she'd been lingering. "I don't think we can help him. He's not in his right mind. Let's keep moving." Renee looked frightened as she took my hand.

As we stepped outside, Hannah caught her breath. "It feels better out here. Ah, I see a man, a soldier. He has a handsome face and expressive eyes. He's looking for someone. I can't hear him, but I can see him quite well."

"That has to be John Belle. He must be looking for his children, maybe Jeopardy. He tried to protect her, I think, but he was killed in an accident." I couldn't help but blurt it out. If Hannah was a fake, she was a good one. There was no way she could know about Loxley and her hand-clapping games. No way at all.

"John? Are you John Belle? My name is Hannah. This is Jerica and Renee. Why are you still here, John?" Hannah clutched her cheap white purse and stared at the empty hallway. "Where are you going? John? We're here to help."

Then the attic door slammed shut, and Renee and I nearly jumped a foot off the ground.

"I think he wants us to follow him." Hannah's light blue eyes widened as she took off down the hallway to the attic door that led up the short stairs to Jeopardy's castle. "Yes, he definitely wants to show us something."

"What do you think, Jerica?" Renee whispered. "Should we go up there?"

"John wouldn't hurt us. I think it's safe if it's him." I didn't bother telling them about how frightened Harper had been up here, how the Lady in White had nearly scared her and Loxley to death. *Maybe it wasn't her. What if it was the angry boy?*

We followed Hannah up the stairs and into the attic. The place seemed so desolate now even though it was stuffed to the brim with boxes and junk. *Where did all this come from?* I brushed my fingers across the top of a dusty box. Did these things belong to Harper? "Jeopardy's bed was over by the window. She liked to watch the moon before she went to sleep," I said to no one in particular. "Jeopardy loved this room. She called it her castle."

"You have a gift, Jerica. Why have you been holding out? How do the visions come to you? When you're awake or asleep? When did they start?"

I swallowed guiltily. "Asleep, mostly, but I have seen a few things awake too. It used to happen a lot when

I was little. I used to dream all the time, but then it stopped. When Marisol...left."

"I hardly ever dream, but I think I would prefer dreams sometimes. Hey, why don't you talk to John? He likes you; I can feel it."

My pulse raced at the thought. "You think I should? I really don't know what to say."

"Try it. What's the worst that can happen?"

I could think of a dozen terrible things that could happen, but I didn't voice them. "JB? Are you here? It was nice meeting you the other day. Do you remember me? I'm Jerica Poole."

I heard a soft whisper, but no words were clear to me. Was I hearing things? Hannah said softly, "He remembers you. Can you hear him?"

I shook my head and said, "Not really." I walked to the window and looked down just as Harper had in my dream the other night. She'd seen Jeopardy with someone. Who had it been? The boy looked a bit like Ray Loper, but she hadn't been sure. "JB, I want to find Jeopardy. I know you tried to protect her. I know you tried to protect them all. Let me help you both. What is it you want me to know?"

Then we heard a strange noise, like scratching. The sound was made by something larger than a rodent. Scratching, clawing. "What is that?" Renee asked breathlessly. Nobody moved for a few minutes. We waited, listening to the scratching, and then it quit. It sounded as if it came from the far wall, near a patch of exposed brickwork. I squatted down and watched in amazement as a small brick tumbled out of the wall. I could see something behind it. I picked up the brick and without thinking poked my fingers in the hole. I couldn't believe it! There was a folded piece of paper in here. No, several papers folded together, like a letter.

I put the brick back in the hole and gazed at Renee and Hannah, who were as amazed as I was. This note belonged to Jeopardy Belle.

Chapter Twenty-One—Jerica

Another shuffling noise surprised me. I ran my hand over another brick and quickly discovered it was loose too. Wiggling it out easily, I found another folded note. Five minutes later, Renee, Hannah and I had recovered five small bundles of paper. As I began to unwrap the first one, I said, "Thank you, JB."

Hannah said quietly, "Wait, I think we should leave now. I am sensing another energy, a young woman, someone different from the woman downstairs. John's presence is waning, and I'm not sure this other one wants us here. In fact, I have a creeping suspicion that she doesn't. Let's leave now. I could use a glass of water anyway."

"Alright." I clutched the bundles protectively as we left Summerleigh. I felt nothing now, nothing except a kind of sad emptiness. Renee breathed a sigh of relief when we stepped outside.

"That whole experience was intense. Thank you, Hannah, and thank you, Jerica, for allowing us inside. I have never experienced anything like that in my life, and I've been to more than a few spooky places."

"You're welcome," I said anxiously. I was ready to get home and read the notes again. It wasn't to be just yet. Jesse was making his way to me. "Hey, what's the word on the roof?" I asked him.

"You called it. It needs to be replaced, and from what I hear from Roger, the other wing needs some serious repair too. What do you have there?"

"Notes, I think. We found them in the attic. They belonged to Jeopardy Belle, I'm sure of it. We're just about to go read them."

Jesse's brown eyes narrowed at hearing my news. "That's incredible. Kind of sorry I missed the investigation now." His phone rang, and he answered it immediately. "Hey, Norm. Yeah, she's right here. You need her?"

He handed the phone to Renee, who frowned at him as if to say, *Couldn't you say I wasn't here?*

"I'm here," she said, walking away from us to take her call. Hannah stared up at the house, her eyes fixed on the nursery window.

"I think at some point you may have to do a cleansing. That boy isn't going to go easily, and he's no less dangerous now than he was in life."

"What boy?" Jesse asked her, giving me a puzzled look.

"I've got to go," Renee said with a sigh. "Norman caught the kitchen on fire, and I've got a mess to tend to. Hannah, if you're riding with me, I'm afraid we'll have to leave now. I've got the fire chief at the diner."

"I'm ready," she said as she tore her gaze from the window. "If you ever need me, Jerica, call me. Don't be afraid to talk to your daughter. She's always near you—just keep her out of Summerleigh."

I couldn't hide my disappointment. I really wanted to ask her more about Marisol, to talk with her at length. "Maybe I could take you home. I don't have anything else to do."

"Yes, you do," she answered cryptically. "But we'll continue this conversation. I promise. We'll talk soon."

Jesse called after Renee, "You need me to tag along?"

"No," she yelled back. "You should probably keep this job at least. I'll call you when I know more."

"Alright," he called back. It was just the two of us now. Even the roofer was leaving.

"Where's he going?"

"I told him to come back after lunch. I have to show you these numbers, and there are a couple of decisions you have to make. We've got to choose a roof color and shingle styles, but I can see you've got other things on your mind."

"Kind of, yes. I'm dying to read these notes. Indulge me a minute or two? I've got some sweet tea in the fridge."

"I'm curious too, and tea sounds great."

Five minutes later, Jesse and I were sitting at my kitchen table carefully unfolding Jeopardy's notes. The ink was a faded blue but not so faded that I couldn't easily read them. Jeopardy's handwriting was slightly slanted except in a few places where the words jumbled with emotion. I began to read the first one, an undated note addressed to her father.

Dear Daddy,

A bluebird sang outside my window today and I threw a rock at him. I couldn't believe it, but I hit that bird. I felt bad when he fell out of the tree dead but not as bad as that bird made me feel singing when you're dead and gone, knowing that I probably killed you by telling you about the Horrible Thing. I am sorry, Daddy. Down to my soul, I am sorry. I wish someone would throw a rock at me!

I buried the bird in a shoe box near your potting shed where you can find him. Maybe you can watch over him, maybe you can bring him back to life and he'll sing for you instead of me. I don't deserve a happy song.

I mean it, Daddy. I wish someone would hit me in the head like that bird. Knock me out cold so I could wake up and be with you every day. I'm not brave enough to do it myself. Carter Hayes' uncle shot himself, but I don't have a gun and I think Momma sold yours. I swim too good to drown. I don't know how I could do it.

But then I worry about what the preacher said and what if dying by your own hand would really send my soul to hell. I would surely never see you again, for you have to be in heaven. Aunt Dot says you are in heaven, all heroes go to heaven, but Loxley says she sees you all the time. I wish I saw you too. I guess you like her more now because she hasn't done any Horrible Things.

I wish I had never told you, I wish I had died instead, Daddy. Maybe Momma's right, I am a Lost Soul.

I need you, Daddy,

Jeopardy Belle

"This is so heartbreaking, Jesse." My hands were shaking as I handed him the note and unfolded another one. "How can she believe that she caused her father's death?"

"Kids think differently. What I want to know is, what's the horrible thing she's talking about? Let's keep reading."

"Okay." I sipped some tea and began to read the second note.

Dear Daddy,

Please come get me, take me where you are! I can't live another day here in Summerleigh. Momma is going to send me to him again, I know she will! And I don't want to go, but she says she will send Harper instead if I don't obey her. What do I do, Daddy?

I thought about something else. What if I killed him so he could never do Horrible Things to anyone again? Wouldn't that be the right thing to do? God would forgive me, I know he would. I have a friend. His name is Troy. You probably remember him...he had the blue spotted hound that used to tear up the garden digging for moles? Well, he's my friend, Daddy, but not my boyfriend even though I know he would like to be. Anyway, he's my friend, and I think he would help me if I told him about the Horrible Thing. He would help me do the deed, but I am afraid. Will I kill him too if I tell him?

Daddy, please answer one of these letters. I have written you so many times, and I don't know what to do. I can't tell Harper or Addison, they'll hate me for sure. Loxley is too little to know about such things. Aunt Dot would never believe me—she always sides with Momma even though Momma hates her too. I don't know what to do. If you don't write me soon or let me see you like Loxley sees you, I will talk to Troy Harvester.

Forgive me, Daddy.

I love you,

Jeopardy Belle

"Troy Harvester? I wonder if she's talking about the old man who owned the tractor supply store in town. He's got to be in his nineties now. I know his granddaughter, Paige. She was part of the Kayla Dickerson benefit I was working with."

"I'm sorry I missed it, but I think I had a heck of a bug." I chewed my fingernail nervously. "I would love to talk to Troy and ask him what he remembers. Hey, come to think of it, how well did you know Ben Hartley?"

"You mean the fellow who used to live here? Not too well, but he was a nice old man. I thought he died a few years ago."

"Well, that's not possible. He's the one who gave me the keys to this place. He came to see Harper the day she died."

"I could be wrong. You know, I might have heard that he moved to the northern part of the state. I'm not sure. You want me to call Paige?"

"Yes. I'll keep reading."

With a nod, Jesse scrolled through his phone and found the number he was looking for. "Hey, Paige? It's me, Jesse. Yeah, I know. Long time no hear from. Renee has kept me busy at the diner." He looked embarrassed but stayed with me. I tried not to be a Nosy Parker. The rest of Jeopardy's letters were much the same as the other two. Whoever this man was, the one who did the "Horrible Things," her mother knew all about it and made every effort to put Jeopardy in his path. I felt sick to my stomach. Who could do such a thing to a child?

"I am working on a story about Jeopardy Belle. I understand your grandfather knew her. I was wondering if my research partner and I could have a few minutes of his time." He waited while she asked.

"Yes, I know it was a long time ago, but it would mean so much. Sure, I'll wait." A minute later, Jesse hung up the phone and said, "Tomorrow at eleven. His place is just outside of town. Anything else in those?"

"Wow, you're good at that. No, and thanks for making that call. I've never been a research partner before," I said with a smile.

"Well, you are now. Or vice versa."

Just then, the roofer pulled into the driveway, and we left the kitchen and Jeopardy's notes to answer his questions. And of course, I had to sign a check. Roger and his crew would come back in the morning to begin working on the roof. I didn't want to go back in the house right now. I needed to work on something, to think about something besides lost Jeopardy and the Horrible Thing she had endured.

"Hey, you want to help me with a small project?"

"Sure, what's that?" Jesse asked curiously.

"I want to clean out the potting shed."

"Okay, Renee will call me when she needs me. Until then, I'm all yours."

I couldn't help but smile at the expression. I wondered what it would be like to be all his...

"It's this way," was my answer. No need to add fuel to a fire that was already burning, at least on my part. It felt good to remember that I was still in the land of the living.

Chapter Twenty-Two—Harper

I expected Momma's fury when I showed her the remnants of her dress, but strangely enough, she didn't blame me at all. She said nothing and gazed up at the ceiling. Jeopardy! Of course she would blame her. But then again, hadn't I? Momma collected the pieces of her dress without a word and left me alone. She didn't offer me another dress, and who could blame her?

"Harper? Why don't you wear the lady's dress? The one from the treasure box in the attic upstairs. I can get it for you if you want me to," Loxley whispered from the doorway.

"That's not my dress, and it wouldn't be right to wear it." Loxley began to cry, and I immediately took her in my arms. "There now, it's not the end of the world. There will be other dances," I lied to her. I never planned on going to another dance again. And if anyone ever nominated me for anything, I would flatly refuse to participate.

"I'm sorry, Harper. I didn't mean it."

"You didn't mean what? What's wrong?"

"Heads up, you two. Aunt Dot is here, and she's got something for you, Harper," Addison's squeaky voice sang happily.

"What do you mean?" I asked Addie.

She leaned against the doorway with her arms crossed. She looked proud of herself, and for the first time in a long time she didn't have pinkeye, a runny nose or a cough. "I called Aunt Dot this morning and told her what Jeopardy did to your dress. She bought you a new dress, a pink one with a little jacket and everything."

"You lie!" I said with a smile.

She crossed her heart as she always did whenever someone accused her of telling a fib. "I never lie. That would send me to the flames. Come see for yourself."

The three of us walked across the Great Room and into the parlor. Aunt Dot was chatting away to Momma, who wasn't saying much. "There she is! Look what we got you!" It was kind of Aunt Dot to pretend that Momma had contributed to this gift. I knew better, but it was a pleasant fiction and I wanted to believe it.

"Oh my goodness! Your hair! Well, we have a few hours to get you fixed up. Try on the dress first. I'm dying to see how it fits."

I couldn't stop smiling as I scurried off to my room and stepped into the satin and tulle dress. I raced down the hall to look in Momma's full-size mirror, and what I saw made me catch my breath. The gown had a sweetheart neckline, and I swear I'd seen one just like it in my magazine. With my head held high, I walked into the parlor and accepted all the compliments. Momma looked mildly pleased as she raised her head from her magazine once or twice, but my sisters were delighted.

After an hour of doctoring my hair and helping me into my stockings and shoes, Aunt Dot clapped her hands at her handiwork. "Now, Cinderella, it's time to head to the ball."

"I'll take her, Dot," Momma said in a dry voice as she stubbed out her cigarette butt in the ashtray. "She's my daughter, after all." My stomach fell, and I couldn't hide my disappointment.

"Oh, I see. Well, alright, but I really didn't mind, Ann. I thought it would be fun."

"No, I think I'll take her. Are you ready, Harper Belle? Where's your jacket? The pink one that Aunt Dot so kindly bought you."

"It's here, Momma."

"Let's go, then. We don't want to be late. Girls, I'll be back soon. Clean up the kitchen. Goodbye, Dot."

"Bye, everyone." Aunt Dot sniffled as she grabbed her hat, gloves and purse and made to leave us. Addison kissed my cheek, but Loxley stayed away as if she were afraid to say goodbye. I walked in a fog, trying to navigate what was happening right now. Later, I would look back and say, *Aha, this is when the warning came*, but at that moment I knew nothing.

"Aunt Dot, you should take her," Jeopardy called from the stairs. Then she headed toward the front door but didn't get too close. She wore her wild hair loose and was dressed like a bohemian, as Momma liked to call her when she wore blue jeans and t-shirts. Tonight she wore a dress and a pair of white high heels she'd borrowed from Momma, no doubt without her permission.

"You have a lot of nerve showing your face tonight, Jeopardy Belle. First, you destroy your sister's dress and now you're trying to ruin her special night? Go to your room!"

The natural smudges under Jeopardy's eyes darkened as they always did when she felt some sort of strong emotion. "You lie! I didn't touch her dress. You probably did it, you mean old..."

"Jeopardy!" Aunt Dot warned her as she scooped up Loxley, who was crying again. "Don't speak to your Momma like that. If you didn't do it, then I believe you, but we don't need to argue and name-call."

"Aunt Dot, don't you let her take Harper anywhere. You have to take her! Please!"

I glanced from her to Momma, unsure what to do—Aunt Dot wasn't sure either. She didn't move, and the five of us stood around the Great Room.

Until we heard the footsteps above us.

I wondered how long we would listen to the sound of heavy footfalls crossing over us. Finally, Momma squinted her eyes at Jeopardy. "You have a boy up there, don't you? Is that who's stomping around upstairs, Jeopardy Belle? That Harvester boy?"

"I ain't got no boy up there, Momma. That's another damn lie!"

Momma's hand flew to Jeopardy's face, and she slapped her hard. Aunt Dot yelled, "Don't hit the girl, Ann!" but it was too late. Jeopardy didn't strike back, just screamed in anger and was gone. She raced through the parlor and then the kitchen. I could hear the screen door slapping behind her.

Momma sagged a little as if it had taken all her energy to slap Jeopardy. "You take her, Dorothy. I'm going to rest a little while. This whole experience has been terrible, just terrible. You see how she treats me! Has any child ever been more disrespectful? She blames me for her father's death, and I just...I don't know..." She began to sob, but nobody moved to help her. Even Aunt Dot didn't try to comfort her.

Aunt Dot whispered to us, "Come on, girls. Let's go." In dramatic fashion, Momma began to weep as she made her way to her favorite parlor chair.

We were in Aunt Dot's car and headed down the road in just a few minutes. That would be the last time I ever saw Jeopardy Belle.

I never even had a chance to say goodbye.

Chapter Twenty-Three—Jerica

"Thank you, Mr. Harvester, for meeting us."

"You're welcome. My granddaughter says you are doing some research about Jeopardy Belle. Do you know how long it's been since I heard anyone say her name? Are you trying to find her?"

"Yes, we would like to find her, Mr. Harvester. I know you cared about her and wanted to help her. I found some notes that she wrote. She mentioned you a few times." I held Jeopardy's faded note in my hand, but he didn't try to take it from me. He didn't say anything at first, but then a sob suddenly escaped his lips.

"Grandpa? Are you okay? Uh, I don't think this is such a good idea. He's been through a lot lately, what with my mother's passing."

"I'm fine. Stop fussing over me like I'm a child, Pat."

She shook her head. "I'm Paige, Grandpa. Pat was my mother."

"You know what I mean. Stop confusing me and make us some coffee, please," he asked her politely in a slightly irritated voice.

She slapped her knees as she got up and said, "Fine. I'll put some coffee on. You guys want some?"

Jesse and I both said yes, and I reminded myself to take my time with this interview. Perhaps I should let the local historian take the lead. I was a nurse and a hobbyist carpenter but certainly no historian. I looked at Jesse as if to say, *You take the lead here.*

"Jerica owns Summerleigh now. Harper left her the house and asked her to continue the search for Jeopardy."

Troy Harvester's eyes were damp with tears, but that news caught his attention. "That's a big place for one person. Do you have a family?"

"Not anymore."

"Oh, I see. I don't have much of one anymore either. Except for Paige. She's a good girl if a little overprotective. Hand me that book there, please." I retrieved the dusty blue vinyl book and handed it to him. He flipped open the photo album and tapped on a black and white photo. I recognized Troy's young face beaming back from the picture. "This was my wife, Elise. We went to school together, but I never even noticed her until our senior year. She never held that against me, and she had a way of loving you completely that made you forget everything else. It was a healing kind of love. Elise had a beautiful voice and an infectious laugh I will never forget. I loved her, I truly did. We had a good life together, better than what I deserved."

"Your granddaughter sure seems fond of you," I said with an encouraging smile.

"She is a feisty young lady like her grandmother was when she was her age." He sighed and shook his head. "You two must think I am an old fool talking about love, but I've been thinking about it a lot lately. Even before I heard you were coming."

"No, we don't," Jesse and I said simultaneously. Mr. Harvester leaned back in his worn cloth recliner and nodded at both of us appreciatively.

"I will never forget that whole horrible year. 1942 was the year Jeopardy disappeared. There she was one moment, larger than life, and then gone. Her disappearance sealed the fate of this town. You see what's left of it. Not much. The war took away many fathers and brothers, and what was left...well, we were a broken community. Desire, Mississippi, didn't amount to much after the war. Most families moved to Mobile for work at the shipyards and others to Lucedale for other types of factory work. My father was a railroad man. He didn't serve in the military long because he had an accident that left him with a limp, but he could still work. Now Mr. Belle, Jeopardy's father, he was a nice enough man, but he could never hold down a job. Back in those days, they didn't label veterans with PTSD and the like. There was no medication. Just booze and whatever mischief you could get into. I think Mr. Belle saw too much. He had those empty eyes, like a lot of men did. I could never understand why he couldn't keep a job. Like I said, he was a nice man, but he was not one to stick to anything. When he won Summerleigh in a card game, he must have thought his luck was changing. He loved those girls of his. He died not long before Jeopardy vanished."

Nobody spoke for a while after that. Troy had poured out a lot of information in lightning fashion, and I was on pins and needles. I wanted to know so much, but Mr. Harvester obviously wasn't going to be rushed.

"Mr. Harvester..."

"Call me Troy."

"Troy, the night Jeopardy disappeared, did you know that she had a fight with Mrs. Belle? She mentioned that something horrible happened to her, a Horrible Thing, she called it." I slid the note toward him hoping he would read it. Again, he didn't try to. Troy closed his eyes and whimpered again. I hated that I would be the one to bring him such pain. It had to be painful to remember all this.

"Yes, the Horrible Thing." His eyes flickered open, and he licked his lips. Paige came in and set a tray of cups, spoons and a sugar bowl on the table. She couldn't hide her worried expression, and she didn't stick around. "I remember the first time I knew I loved her. We were at the river, my brothers and I. My oldest brother, Anthony—everyone called him Tony—he liked to ride to the river after church on Sundays. Harry and I didn't want to be left behind. It was a rare thing for a teenage boy to have a car in our small town, and it was nice to be noticed. Tony was a popular boy. The girls were always circling around him...that day was no exception. That particular day he tried putting the moves on one of those Taylor girls, but she wasn't having any of it. I got tired of watching him act stupid.

"Harry and I were in the water when Jeopardy came down the bank. I don't think she noticed me at all. She walked into the water wearing a white dress like she was headed to a baptism. After she waded out about waist deep, she closed her eyes like she was saying a prayer and then sank down in the water until it covered her head. I don't know that anyone else saw her, but I did. Everything stood still as I waited for her to come back up. Do you believe in magic?"

I nodded, and Jesse did too.

"That was some kind of magic. I will never forget the sight of her. I watched and waited, and just when I thought the worst, that she drowned herself in Dog River, she burst out of the water like some kind of siren, slinging her hair behind her. Her hands slid over her face and brushed the water away, and then she stared at me with those sad, hazel eyes and said, 'What exactly are you staring at, Troy Harvester?' I could hardly believe it—she knew my name! From that day to this one, I have loved her with all my heart."

"Oh, Troy, she loved you too," I blurted out. "I know she did."

"In her way, perhaps. Jeopardy Belle was a summer storm, and I was a trusty rock that she battered against when she needed someone, which was rarely. I was so young; I didn't know how to help her. All I knew was I loved her."

I sighed hearing Troy's account of Jeopardy, and then he surprised me by adding, "I saw her that night after she left Summerleigh. I never told any-one that, but I should have. She came to my house and stayed with me. I went to sleep, and when I woke up, she was gone."

"What? You saw Jeopardy that night? I don't re-member reading that in the police report," Jesse said. "Are you sure, Troy?"

"Yes, I saw her. No one but me."

Paige reappeared with a pot of coffee, which she placed on the trivet in front of me. Eyeing us suspi-ciously, she disappeared to the kitchen again. I knew she was listening. I would too if I were her.

"I was already asleep when she tapped on my win-dow. My room was over the garage, but she didn't come up the stairs. She climbed up the wisteria vine like a wild creature. My brothers had gone to the school dance, but I stayed home. I didn't have the courage to ask Jeopardy to go, and I didn't want to see her dancing with either of my brothers. She liked to kiss Tony on the cheek; I used to think that was because she knew it bothered me. I don't know. Sometime that night, I heard fingers tapping on my window. It was Jeopardy, soaked to the bone. I thought I was dreaming. Imagine seeing the girl you loved with all your might tapping on your window.

"'What are you doing here, Jeopardy Belle?' I asked as I rubbed my eyes to make sure I wasn't dreaming. She didn't answer me, and I held my hand out to her to help her in. I closed the window behind her, raced to the rocking chair for my extra blanket and wrapped it around her.

"'Warm me up, Troy Harvester. I'm so cold,' she said.

"'What are you doing here? Are you alright?' I asked. I pushed her wet hair out of her face. I wondered if she'd had a fall or something; she had a purple bruise on the side of her face.

"'No, nothing is right. Nothing at all, Troy.' She laid her head on my shoulder. I don't know how long we sat there. Then she asked, 'Do you have any food? I am so hungry.'

"I told her I could make her a sandwich and asked if she liked peanut butter. She said yes, so I told her to stay there and dry off. 'Where else am I going to go?' she asked.

"I raced down the stairs and into the main house to make Jeopardy a sandwich. My grandmother was in the front room listening to her radio program. She saw me but didn't think my ransacking the kitchen was strange. My parents were already in their beds, and my brothers wouldn't be home until much later. A few minutes later, I hurried back to my room. I was so worried she would be gone, but she hadn't gone anywhere. During my absence, she'd helped herself to a pair of my jeans and a jersey that was far too big for her. Her wet dress was draped over the back of my desk chair. I stepped inside with the sandwich and brought it to her like her obedient servant.

"'Don't forget the milk,' I instructed her politely. She ate half the sandwich, chugged down the milk and crawled into my bed. I didn't know what to do. I'd never had a girl in my room and certainly not one in my bed. I picked up the plate and glass and put them on my desk.

"Without being asked, I crawled back in my bed and lay on my pillow uneasily. Jeopardy curled up to me with her head on my chest. That was the happiest moment of my life. She smelled like sweat and rain, like cotton and peanut butter. God, I loved her.

"Then she said, 'A Horrible Thing happened to me, Troy, and it's going to happen again. Pray with me. Pray that Daddy comes and takes me away.'

"I said to her, 'Your father is gone, Jeopardy. You can't go with him; that means you'll be dead.'"

I had to ask, "What horrible thing was she talking about, Troy?"

I wasn't sure he heard me because he didn't answer me. He said, "I don't know why, but I suddenly had the courage to tell her how I felt. I was completely unaware of how much she needed me. I just blurted it all out without fear. I told her, 'You know I love you, Jeopardy. I have always loved you. Don't you kiss another boy from this moment on, you hear? You climbed up into my bedroom, and now we're here together. You're my girl, Jeopardy Belle. Promise me we'll always be together.'

"'I promise, Troy Harvester,' she swore as I held her close and she clung even tighter. We didn't do anything beyond that; she didn't need me pawing at her. When I woke up, she had changed her clothes and left my jeans and shirt behind. And I never saw her again. Never, and I waited every night." Troy burst into tears. "She needed me, and I let her down. I knew she was in trouble, and I couldn't help her. Now she's gone!" He covered his eyes with one hand and sobbed as Paige came back.

She said softly, "I'm afraid you'll have to leave. That's enough, please."

"I am so sorry, Troy. Yes, we'll leave, Paige. Thank you."

We walked out of the Harvester home and drove back to the cottage in silence. Jesse and I didn't talk much on the way, and he didn't stick around to chat. He had to meet Renee, something to do with the fire damage.

I politely thanked him for the ride and went inside.

Someone was waiting for me.

Chapter Twenty-Four—Jeopardy Belle

Troy Harvester slept through my kiss. I didn't want to leave him, but I couldn't stay here and bring my misery down upon him. Troy was right—I was his girl. I always had been, but I couldn't tell him anything. He didn't deserve it. When I came to the Harvesters' house, I had every intention of asking Troy for a gun. Just a small gun that I could use one time, and then I'd give it back to him. But then he told me he loved me, and how much he loved me, and all that changed.

I loved Troy Harvester almost as much as I loved Harper and Daddy and Addison and Loxley. Too much to get him into trouble. When I shimmied down the wisteria vine, I had no idea what I would do. All I could do was go back to Summerleigh, maybe sleep in Daddy's potting shed until I could sneak back into the house. When I didn't have to see Momma, when I knew she wouldn't come after me.

She'd hated me all my life, and I didn't know why. I couldn't understand it. For a long time, I did everything right. I said ma'am and please, I made good grades in school, cleaned my room, tended the garden...but it didn't matter. She never saw any of it, so I quit. I quit trying and she noticed me then, but she still didn't love me. Not even a little bit.

What made it worse was she wanted Daddy to hate me too. She wanted everyone to hate me. I think most everyone did, but I didn't care. Daddy loved me until the day he died. He told me he did; he promised he did even when I told him about the Horrible Thing.

He was so mad, but not at me, he said. "You're my daughter, Jeopardy Belle. You always will be. I'll make this right. I'll take care of this, Jeopardy."

"I'm sorry, Daddy. I didn't mean for any of this to happen."

"You don't have a thing to be sorry about." He held me as I cried out my heart and soul. I remembered how strong he felt. He kissed the top of my head and told me to wait for him. "I'll be back soon."

"Okay, Daddy."

But he never came back, except as a ghost.

No, I wasn't sure what I would do when I began walking down Hurlette Drive, down to Summerleigh, but then I saw a white rock in the road. I remembered the bird I'd killed accidentally. Maybe if I hit Grandpa Daughdrill with a rock, he would die too. I picked up the rock and put it in my purse. Yes, that's what I would do. I would hit him, once, twice, maybe three times if need be. And then everyone would know what a Horrible Man he was and what Horrible Things he did to me.

I was almost home now. The sun would be coming up soon. And then I saw the lights coming down the road. Those were the lights of a Master DeLuxe. Grandpa Daughdrill had one, and so did Momma. They bought them together, and I think Grandpa gave her the gift in exchange for me. He never told me that, but he promised me many things and he always gave me money afterward. I hadn't spent any of it, except to buy cigarettes.

How strange that I wasn't allowed to call him Grandpa until after the Horrible Thing. "None of your sisters can call me that. Only you, sweet Jeopardy. My special girl. Just like your Momma. She was always my favorite, like you."

I cried as he told me these Horrible Secrets. And then he pawed at me and I floated away and thought about swimming in the river until it was over. And now he was coming again. That had to be him. I dug my hand in my purse and held the rock.

My grandfather pulled up beside me and rolled down the window. "Get in the car, girl. Your mother is worried about you. What do you mean running out of the house like that?" I didn't answer him but obediently got into his car. I started to get in the front seat, but he shook his head and clucked his tongue. "No, you ride in the back seat. I am afraid you'll have to be punished, Jeopardy."

"I haven't done anything wrong," I said with my hand still on the rock. Panic rose in me. I didn't want this! Why had I gotten in his car? I couldn't have run from him; he was too tall and big and strong. I started to cry, and he began to scold me and threaten me. Suddenly, I took the rock and banged it against the window and glass shattered everywhere. I was getting out of this car one way or another.

He swore at me and the car stopped. I reached my hand outside and opened the door. I tumbled out but not fast enough; Grandpa Daughdrill was grabbing me off the ground, and I started to scream. His hand clasped my mouth, and I kicked and punched him. I'd lost my rock but managed to grab it again before he carried me off into the woods behind Summerleigh.

"No! You won't touch me again!" I screamed behind his hand. I even bit it. He snatched his hand away because of the pain, and I screamed at the top of my lungs, "Daddy! Help me!" I hit Grandpa Daughdrill in the head with my rock, and he hit the ground.

But he didn't stay down. He got back up, and I began to cry as he staggered on his feet. "You little bitch! You'll pay for that. I'm done with you, Jeopardy Belle. It's time to find a new favorite!" He hit me like a man and knocked me out. When I woke up, I was bound and gagged and in a sack. I must be in the trunk of his car. I heard a woman's voice too. Was that Momma? I kicked around in the trunk of the Master DeLuxe and screamed through the gag. Nobody could hear me, but I had to try.

Finally, when I grew tired, I heard the voices again, outside the trunk now. "It was an accident, Ann. She went wild, there was no reasoning with her. I think she was drunk, or something. She fell and hit her head. She's dead."

"No, that can't be right. She can't be dead. I never meant for her to die. Father, how could you do this?"

"Now, now, Ann. You know your father would never do anything to hurt you or Jeopardy. Trust me. I'll take care of her body, but you have to keep quiet, no matter what."

"Okay, Father. I will let you handle it."

"Good girl, Ann. Now go home. Go home and take care of your girls. Jeopardy is mine."

I twisted and kicked in the bag, but nobody heard me. Then the trunk opened, and light filtered through the rough burlap bag I was in. Grandpa Daughdrill picked me up and took me somewhere. Where? I could smell pine and rain. I kicked, but he said, "Shh...it's too late now. You are a great disappointment to me. I have something to tell you, Jeopardy. You aren't a Belle at all. You're my daughter. All mine. That man, John Jeffrey Belle, he was nothing to you. I was your father, all the time. I wanted you to know that before you die."

I cried and screamed but couldn't talk. My mind screamed at him, railing against him, but then I heard the gun cock and I knew what was about to happen. My prayers had been answered. I was about to die, and it wouldn't be by my own hand. Grandpa thought he was punishing me, but he was really setting me free. I would be free to be with Daddy. My own Daddy!

I didn't hear the gunshot. Suddenly, I wasn't in the bag but standing beside it, watching Grandpa's grim face. He picked up the bloody sack, tied rocks to it with ropes and carried me out into my precious Dog River and sank me beneath a log.

I didn't feel sadness. I felt free, and I wanted to go home now. Home to Daddy. I walked along the road, and nobody saw me. I walked up to the door at Summerleigh, but I could not get in. The door wouldn't open! I walked around to the back door too but couldn't get in there either.

A little boy was in there, an angry boy. He told me my Daddy was here at Summerleigh, but he was his Daddy now. He wanted me to go away. He was strong, so strong that he could keep me out forever. And he said with an evil smile that Momma would die soon too, and he would make sure she would never let me in. He laughed at me, and I walked toward the potting shed. I turned back once and saw my Daddy upstairs. He couldn't come to me, and I couldn't go to him.

I didn't think dead people cried, but I did. I cried because even after everything, I couldn't be with Daddy.

We would be apart forever.

***

I woke up immediately and called Jesse. It was after eleven o'clock, but who else could I tell? "Hey, Jesse. I had a dream. I saw Jeopardy Belle...I know who killed her. I know where she is."

"I'm on the way."

Five hours later, the George County Sheriff Department was searching for her body. It took them only four hours to find her. I cried the whole time. Jesse held me, and I didn't care that I hardly knew him. He was here and I needed him, just like Jeopardy needed Troy.

When it was over with, we went home and Jesse persuaded me to eat by whipping up his famed Double Slam. I didn't eat much, but it was nice to have someone care for me. I needed it.

I walked outside after supper and stared up at the attic window. "I wonder if he's there right now, just watching and waiting for Jeopardy."

"She's not far. She's in the potting shed."

"We have to bring them together, Jesse. We have to!"

"I'll call Hannah and Renee. Let's bring them in, and they can tell us how to do it."

"Okay, sounds good to me."

Jesse hugged me, and I loved every second of it. "You're amazing, Jerica Poole. You found her even when everyone else had failed. You did it."

"I think it was just time, and Harper helped a lot. All I had to do was put the pieces together."

"So, is your work done here?"

"No, we're just getting started. There are two other ghosts at Summerleigh. They deserve to be at peace. All we have to do is..."

"I know, put the pieces together. Do you do this all the time, Jerica?"

"No, I'm a nurse. Not a psychic or anything else."

"You're a mom and a sensitive, I'd say. Are you sure you aren't a cook too? We could use a hand at the diner," he said with a wink.

"Definitely not," I replied with a laugh. "One more thing, Jesse Clarke. I like you."

"I like you too, Jerica. I'm hoping to get to know you better."

I liked hearing that. I smiled and said, "Well then, stick around. We're just getting started."

Epilogue—Jerica

"Now, Jerica. Tell her what you know," Hannah said as she held my hand firmly. "We have to reveal her secret or she'll never leave."

"Ann Belle, I know—no, we know—what you did. I know what you did to Jeopardy." The dusty red velvet couch shifted a few inches. "Did you see that?"

"Don't let her scare you. Stand your ground, Jerica. This is the only way Jeopardy and John will ever be reunited. Ann has to move on," Renee said in a soft voice. I glanced at Jesse, who watched me protectively. At least I wasn't doing this by myself.

"Okay," I said as I held hands with Renee and Hannah even tighter. "I'm sorry for what was done to you, I am sorry your own father was such a horrible man. I know what he did, but what you're doing isn't right." The couch bumped again, and I heard footsteps upstairs; they sounded like heavy boots. Hannah looked troubled, but I pretended not to notice. I kept talking. I had to get through to Ann. She had to let Jeopardy come home!

"Ann, you can't change what you did in life, but you can change what you're doing right now!"

The front door flew open, and an evil wind blew in blasts of wet leaves. "Keep going," Hannah encouraged me.

"Ann, the secret is out. All the secrets. You can't hide them anymore!" The chandelier above us began to sway, and the footsteps upstairs sounded louder and close. Were they coming down the stairs?

"You can't hide it anymore! We know the truth!" Tears streamed down my face now. Images of Marisol flashed through my head. My baby's smiling face as I stuck my tongue out at her in the rearview mirror that moment before the crash. Her cries for me when the truck struck us, the absolute silence when the train hit us. My own Horrible Thing.

"I know the truth, Ann. You can't always protect your children, even though you want to more than anything." The door slammed shut, and the leaves fell around us. I closed my eyes, determined to stay focused. "But you can't blame Jeopardy for what happened to you. I know if she could, she would forgive you, Ann. She would forgive you with all her heart."

And suddenly everything stopped.

"She's gone. You did it, Jerica. Ann is gone."

I opened my eyes again, and everyone except Jesse was crying; he was staring at something over my shoulder. "Holy heck! That's John," he said.

We all looked at the staircase, and sure enough, an apparition appeared. It was solid for a few seconds, then it faded, but I could still see him standing there waiting for something. No, someone.

The front door of Summerleigh opened slowly. No more wind, no more leaves and swaying chandelier.

Everything was calm now. I didn't see her, but I could feel her.

Jeopardy Belle was home! A warm breeze pushed past us, and my hair fluttered as the breeze blew up the stairs. The strips of wallpaper fluttered with her passing. They were together now, Jeopardy and her Daddy. The place felt lighter, and it was easier to breathe.

They would always be together.

Read on for an excerpt from the next book
in the series,

The Ghost of Jeopardy Belle

"Momma, Loxley is talking to her ghosts again," Addison announced sourly. The three of us girls were in the parlor reading the magazines that Mrs. Hendrickson gave me after her granddaughter left them behind when she returned to Mobile, but Addie was in a bad mood. Mostly because Loxley refused to move out of her current spot on the couch. Their bickering frustrated me. I wanted to finish this article about dreamy Frank Sinatra. I loved all his songs, especially Stardust, and I thought it might be a hoot to start a fan club right here in Desire. Other girls liked him too, but only I knew all his songs by heart. Whenever one of Sinatra's songs came on the radio, I sang it with all my might. I'd been saving up to buy a few of his records, maybe a whole album, but my record player would need a new needle soon. Aunt Dot gave me her RCA Victor because she bought herself a Wellington record player and radio for her birthday. It played three speeds and had a shiny wooden case. That was the last time I'd seen Aunt Dot, weeks ago. I missed her.

"Addison, stop," I warned her again in a whisper. My sister rubbed her nose with a hankie, but it didn't do much good. Her nose ran perpetually nowadays. Probably because it had rained for a whole week straight. Any kind of mold made her sick, and there were plenty of moldy spots in the old plantation we called home. Although I felt sympathy for her, I wished she would heed my warning. Instead, it appeared that her ill mood and Loxley's mischievousness would put us all in harm's way.

"No, I wasn't, Momma," Loxley called out innocently. "I was talking to Lenny, my pet."

"You girls keep quiet in there," Miss Augustine barked at us as she and Momma continued their gossiping and gin drinking and card playing at the kitchen table. I peeked around the corner from my spot on the floor. No, Momma wasn't moving, and she looked terrible today. Ever since Jeopardy's disappearance, something about her seemed wrong. Ann Marie Belle had always been a proud, pretty woman, beautiful like a model. Not anymore. She wore too much makeup, so much that it bordered on clownish, and she often had lipstick on her teeth. Her blond hair showed dark roots, and today she was still wearing her robe and pajamas. That was unheard of around here. Momma had always been the first one up in the morning and always dressed to the nines like a proper lady, especially on Sundays. But we didn't go to church anymore, and no one from First Baptist came to visit us. It was as if we were living on an island here at Summerleigh.

"Want to see my pet, Addison? I'll show you he's real." Loxley hopped off the loveseat but didn't budge from in front of it. With a perfectly innocent smile, she held out a pocket of her pinafore and offered Addison a peek inside.

Addie rubbed her nose again and waved her away. Her pale face crumpled miserably, and although she spent much of her time in bed, I thought perhaps she really needed to go for a lie-down. "Take your pet outside and give me my spot back, Loxley."

Loxley poked out her bottom lip and stomped her foot. "It's not your spot. I don't see your name on it. Isn't that right, Harper?" I didn't offer her any help. She was only making matters worse. I flipped the page of the magazine and tried to ignore them both. "Don't you want to see Lenny, Addison?"

Before Addison could reply, a green tree frog with big red eyes hopped out of Loxley's pocket and onto Addison's shoe. Addie screamed, and before I knew what was happening Momma stormed into the room with Miss Augustine in tow. Momma grabbed me first, picking me up by my hair, uncaring that I had nothing to do with the hoopla. Miss Augustine scolded her, "Now, Ann. Calm down. Remember what the doctor said about your nerves." But Momma didn't listen. She swung at my behind with her free hand, striking me not once but three times before she let me go. I yelped in surprise and pain while my sisters scrambled up the stairs.

"I told you to keep those girls quiet! Why don't you ever listen to me, Harper? You never listen!"

"I'm sorry, Momma. I'm sorry!" I yelled back, shocked at her violent attack. Miss Augustine stepped back and watched us from the doorway as if she too were afraid of Momma. Momma stomped toward me while I tried to back away. It was no use. There was no sense in fighting her, and I couldn't bring myself to raise a hand back. I closed my eyes and waited for the blow, thinking she'd slap me across the face. She liked doing that when I spoke an ill word to her. Or what she considered an ill word. A knock on the door put a stop to her intentions, and she squeezed my arm one good time before releasing me and tidying her robe. Without waiting to see who had arrived, I raced up the stairs to hide. The creaking floors moaned at my steps, but that did not slow me down. It was at that moment I decided Jeopardy's castle would become my castle, at least until she came home.

I ran up the attic stairs and closed the door behind me, tears streaming down my face. I didn't know where Addison was, but Loxley sat on Jeopardy's pallet crying for all she was worth. Her pretty face was streaked with dirty tears; her usually tidy braids were sagging in the heat of the attic.

"I'm sorry, Harper. I didn't know Lenny would jump out. He's never done that before. He's a good frog. Honest he is." I collapsed on the pallet and covered my face with my hands. My broken heart weighed heavy in my chest like a ton of lead. Even though she was the baby of the family, Loxley held me as I cried. After a few minutes of stroking my hair, she said, "I'm sorry, Harper. Really, I am. Did she hurt you real bad?" Her eyes were fearful and full of tears.

For her sake, I lied, "Not too bad." I sat up now and did what older sisters were supposed to do. I comforted Loxley, and we held one another a few minutes. "Loxley, tell me the truth. Do you ever see Jeopardy? I have to know. Is Jeopardy here...is she a ghost?"

Loxley slowly shook her head. "I never see Jeopardy, but I look for her, Harper. Honest, I have tried. Daddy comes sometimes, but he doesn't talk to me. I can see his mouth moving, but I can't hear him. He looks sad now. And he doesn't smile anymore."

"Is he...does he look like he always did?" *He's not bloody, is he? Tell me he doesn't look like a bloody fiend.*

"Yes, he looks the same." She wrinkled her neat blond brows and said, "But he's not the only one here."

"The lady ghost? Do you see her?"

"Not much, but the other night I heard tapping on my window." She tapped at the air. "It was real soft, like how Jeopardy used to tap on your window when she wanted to come inside. But when I got up to look for Jeopardy, it was just the boy, the mean one who comes around sometimes. He used to stay upstairs, but now he goes all over the place, even outside. He has black eyes, Harper, and he scares me. He scratches me sometimes."

I didn't have any sisterly advice, so I just nodded thoughtfully, and suddenly her eyes brimmed with tears again. "He...he made me cut up your dress, Harper. I'm so sorry. He said I had to do it or something horrible would happen to you. He gave me the scissors."

Stunned at her confession, I held her and said nothing else. All this time, I had believed that Jeopardy had destroyed the dress Momma had let me borrow for the Harvest Dance. I believed that Jeopardy wanted to hurt me, and she'd been innocent the whole time. Loxley and I both gasped as the attic door creaked open, but it was only Addison who stepped inside. I waved at her to join us on the pallet.

She didn't say, "I'm sorry." Addison rarely apologized, but just her being here was proof of her repentance. I held her too, and the three of us sobbed together until we were all cried out. I opened the window to cool the room, and soon my sisters and I fell asleep. No one came to look for us. Not like the day Aunt Dot came to tell us that Daddy had died. I shuddered to think of him bleeding out pinned inside his old truck. Momma didn't like coming up here, not since that ghost pushed her down the stairs. And I knew it was a ghost because I'd seen her with my own two eyes. The door hung open for a while and didn't move again. But just as I closed my eyes, I saw the door open wider.

"Jeopardy?" I asked as sleep took me under. It was then that I saw him. I hovered between sleep and wakefulness, and I was unable to move or speak. I couldn't cry out or warn my sisters. It was as if I were paralyzed. At first, I saw a black form—blacker than a crow's wing, blacker than the darkness that enveloped the attic. But then the blackness became something else. It was a gray mist and had a shape, a boy's shape. And now, by some strange magic, I could see him clear as day.

He stared at me with perfect hatred, and then a black smile crossed his face.

More from M. L. Bullock

From the *Ultimate Seven Sisters Collection*

A smile crept across my face when I turned back to look at the pale faces watching me from behind the lace curtains of the girls' dormitory. I didn't feel sorry for any of them—all of those girls hated me. They thought they were my betters because they were orphans and I was merely the accidental result of my wealthy mother's indiscretion. I couldn't understand why they felt that way. As I told Marie Bettencourt, at least my parents were alive and wealthy. Hers were dead and in the cold, cold ground. "Worm food now, I suppose." Her big dark eyes had swollen with tears, her ugly, fat face contorting as she cried. Mrs. Bedford scolded me for my remarks, but even that did not worry me.

I had a tool much more effective than Mrs. Bedford's threats of letters to the attorney who distributed my allowance or a day without a meal. Mr. Bedford would defend me—for a price. I would have to kiss his thin, dry lips and pretend that he did not peek at my décolletage a little too long. Once he even squeezed my bosom ever so quickly with his rough hands but then pretended it had been an accident. Mr. Bedford never had the courage to lift up my skirt or ask me for a "discreet favor," as my previous chaperone had called it, but I enjoyed making him stare. It had been great fun for a month or two until I saw how easily he could be manipulated.

And now my rescuer had come at last, a man, Louis Beaumont, who claimed to be my mother's brother. I had never met Olivia, my mother. Not that I could remember, anyway, and I assumed I never would.

Louis Beaumont towered above most men, as tall as an otherworldly prince. He had beautiful blond hair that I wanted to plunge my hands into. It looked like the down of a baby duckling. He had fair skin—so light it almost glowed—with pleasant features, even brows, thick lashes, a manly mouth. It was a shame he was so near a kin because I would have had no objections to whispering "Embrasse-moi" in his ear. Although I very much doubted Uncle Louis would have indulged my fantasy. How I loved to kiss, and to kiss one so beautiful! That would be heavenly. I had never kissed a handsome man before—I kissed the ice boy once and a farmhand, but neither of them had been handsome or good at kissing.

For three days we traveled in the coach, my uncle explaining what he wanted and how I would benefit if I followed his instructions. According to my uncle, Cousin Calpurnia needed me, or rather, needed a companion for the season. The heiress would come out this year, and a certain level of decorum was expected, including traveling with a suitable companion. "Who would be more suitable than her own cousin?" he asked me with the curl of a smile on his regal face. "Now, dearest Isla," he said, "I am counting on you to be a respectable girl. Leave all that happened before behind in Birmingham—no talking of the Bedfords or anyone else from that life. All will be well now." He patted my hand gently. "We must find Calpurnia a suitable husband, one that will give her the life she's accustomed to and deserves."

Yes, indeed. Now that this Calpurnia needed a proper companion, I had been summoned. I'd never even heard of Miss Calpurnia Cottonwood until now. Where had Uncle Louis been when I ran sobbing in a crumpled dress after falling prey to the lecherous hands of General Harper, my first guardian? Where had he been when I endured the shame and pain of my stolen maidenhead? Where? Was I not Beaumont stock and worthy of rescue? Apparently not. I decided then and there to hate my cousin, no matter how rich she was. Still, I smiled, spreading the skirt of my purple dress neatly around me on the seat. "Yes, Uncle Louis."

"And who knows, ma petite Cherie, perhaps we can find you a good match too. Perhaps a military man or a wealthy merchant. Would you like that?" I gave him another smile and nod before I pretended to be distracted by something out the window. My fate would be in my own hands, that much I knew. Never would I marry. I would make my own future. Calpurnia must be a pitiful, ridiculous kind of girl if she needed my help to land a "suitable" husband with all her affluence.

About the *Ultimate Seven Sisters Collection*

When historian Carrie Jo Jardine accepted her dream job as chief historian at Seven Sisters in Mobile, Alabama, she had no idea what she would encounter. The moldering old plantation housed more than a few boxes of antebellum artifacts and forgotten oil paintings. Secrets lived there—and they demanded to be set free.

This contains the entire supernatural suspense series.

More from M. L. Bullock

From *The Ghosts of Idlewood*

I arrived at Idlewood at seven o'clock thinking I'd have plenty of time to mark the doors with taped signs before the various contractors arrived. There was no electricity, so I wasn't sure what the workmen would actually accomplish today. I'd dressed down this morning in worn blue jeans and a long-sleeved t-shirt. It just felt like that kind of day. The house smelled stale, and it was cool but not freezing. We'd enjoyed a mild February this year, but like they say, "If you don't like the weather in Mobile, just wait a few minutes."

I really hated February. It was "the month of love," and this year I wasn't feeling much like celebrating. I'd given Chip the heave-ho for good right after Christmas, and our friendship hadn't survived the breakup. I hated that because I really did like him as a person, even if he could be narrow-minded about spiritual subjects. I hadn't been seeing anyone, but I was almost ready to get back into the dating game. Almost.

I changed out the batteries in my camera before beginning to document the house. Carrie Jo liked having before, during and after shots of every room.

According to the planning sheet Carrie Jo and I developed last month, all the stage one doors were marked. On her jobs, CJ orchestrated everything:

what rooms got painted first, where the computers would go, which room we would store supplies in, that sort of thing. I also put no-entry signs on rooms that weren't safe or were off-limits to curious workers. The home was mostly empty, but there were some pricy mantelpieces and other components that would fetch a fair price if you knew where to unload stolen items such as high-end antiques. Surprisingly, many people did.

I'd start the pictures on the top floor and work my way down. I peeked out the front door quickly to see if CJ was here. No sign of her yet, which wasn't like her at all. She was usually the early bird. I smiled, feeling good that Carrie Jo trusted me enough to give me the keys to this grand old place. There were three floors, although the attic space wasn't a real priority for our project. The windows would be changed, the floors and roof inspected, but not a lot of cosmetic changes were planned for up there beyond that. We'd prepare it for future storage of seasonal decorations and miscellaneous supplies. Seemed a waste to me. I liked the attic; it was roomy, like an amazing loft apartment. But it was no surprise I was drawn to it—when I was a kid, I practically lived in my tree house.

I stuffed my cell phone in my pocket and jogged up the wide staircase in the foyer. I could hear birds chirping upstairs; they probably flew in through a broken window. There were quite a few of them from the sound of it. Since I hadn't labeled any doors upstairs or in the attic, I hadn't had the opportunity to explore much up there. It felt strangely exhilarating to do so all by myself. The first flight of stairs appeared safe, but I took my time on the next two. Water damage wasn't always easy to spot, and I had no desire to fall through a weak floor. When I reached the top of the stairs to the attic, I turned the knob and was surprised to find it locked.

"What?" I twisted it again and leaned against the door this time, but it wouldn't move. I didn't see a keyhole, so that meant it wasn't locked after all. I supposed it was merely stuck, the wood probably swollen from moisture. "Rats," I said. I set my jaw and tried one last time. The third time must have been the charm because it opened freely, as if it hadn't given me a world of problems before. I nearly fell as it gave way, laughing at myself as I regained my balance quickly. I reached for my camera and flipped it to the video setting. I panned the room to record the contents. There were quite a few old trunks, boxes and even the obligatory dressmaker's dummy. It was a nerd girl historian's dream come true.

Like an amateur documentarian, I spoke to the camera: "Maiden voyage into the attic at Idlewood. Today is February 4th. This is Rachel Kowalski recording."

Rachel Kowalski recording, something whispered back. My back straightened, and the fine hairs on my arms lifted as if to alert me to the presence of someone or something unseen.

I froze and said, "Hello?" I was happy to hear my voice and my voice alone echo back to me.

Hello?

About *The Ghosts of Idlewood*

When a team of historians takes on the task of restoring the Idlewood plantation to its former glory, they discover there's more to the moldering old home than meets the eye. The long-dead Ferguson children don't seem to know they're dead. A mysterious clock, a devilish fog and the Shadow Man add to the supernatural tension that begins to build in the house. Lead historian Carrie Jo Stuart and her assistant Rachel must use their special abilities to get to the bottom of the many mysteries that the house holds.

Detra Ann and Henri get a reality check, of the supernatural kind, and Deidre Jardine finally comes face to face with the past.

More from M. L. Bullock

From *The Ghosts of Kali Oka Road*

"Sierra to base."

Sara's well-manicured nails wrapped around the black walkie-talkie. "This is base. Go ahead, Sierra."

"Five minutes. No sign of the client. K2 is even Steven. Temp is 58F."

"Great. Check back in five. Radio silence, please."

"All right."

She tapped the antenna of the walkie-talkie to her chin. "I hope she remembers to take pictures. Did she take her camera?" she asked Midas. It was the first time she'd spoken to him this afternoon.

"Yes, but it wouldn't hurt to have a backup. You have yours?"

Sara cocked an eyebrow at him. "Are you kidding? I'm no rookie." She cast a stinging look of disdain in my direction and strolled back to her car in her stylish brown boots and began searching her back seat, presumably for her camera.

"Am I missing something?" I couldn't help but ask. The uncomfortable feeling kept rising. I'd had enough weirdness for one day.

Nobody answered me. Midas glared after Sara, but it was Peter who broke the silence.

"Cassidy, have you always been interested in the supernatural? Seems like we all have our own stories to tell. All of us have either seen something or lost someone. They say the loss of a loved one in a tragic way makes you more sensitive to the spirit world. I think that might be true."

"You're an ass, Pete. You're joking about her sister? She doesn't know she's lost her." I could see Midas' muscles ripple under his shirt. He wore a navy blue sweater, the thin, fitted kind that had three buttons at the top.

"I'm sorry, Cassidy. I swear to you I'm not a heartless beast."

"How could you not know?" Sara scolded him. "She told us about her the other night."

"I had my headphones on half the time, cueing up video and photographs. Shoot. I'm really sorry, Cassie."

That was the last straw. I was about to tell him how I really felt about his "joke." I took a deep breath and said, "My name is Cassidy, and..."

The walkie-talkie squawked, and I heard Sierra's voice, "Hey! Y'all need to get in here, now!"

Immediately everyone began running toward the narrow pathway. Midas snatched the walkie. "Sierra! What's up?"

"Someone's out here—stalking us."

"Can you see who it is? Is it Ranger?"

"Definitely not! Footsteps are too fast for someone so sick." Her whisper sent a shiver down my spine. "I'm taking pictures...should we keep pushing in toward the house?"

"Yes, keep going. We're double-timing your way. Stay on the path, Sierra. Don't get lost. Follow your GPS. It should lead you right to it."

"Okay."

"Midas! Let's flank whoever this is!" Pete said, his anger rising.

Midas looked at me as if to say, "Are you going to be all right?"

Sara said, "Go and help Sierra. Cassidy and I will follow."

Immediately Midas took off to the left and Peter to the right. They flanked the narrow road and scurried through the woods to see if they could detect the intruder.

Sara handed me her audio recorder. "Hold this! I'm grabbing some photos. We're going to run, Cassidy. I hope you can keep up."

"Sure, I used to run marathons." I didn't want to seem like a wimp. Now didn't seem like the time to tell her that I hadn't trained in over six months. "But why are we running? Are they in danger, do you think? Maybe it's just a homeless person."

"The element of surprise! Hit record and come on! Get your ass in gear, girl!"

I pressed the record button, gritted my teeth and took off after her. We ran down the leaf-littered path; the afternoon sunlight was casting lean shadows in a few spots now. We'd be out of sun soon. Then we'd be running through the woods in the dark. Was it supposed to be this cold out here?

I wish I held the temperature thingy instead, but I didn't.

"You feel that, Cassidy? The cold?" She bounded over a log in front of me, and I followed her. "Not unusual for the woods, but this is more than that," she said breathlessly. "I think it might mean we've got supernatural activity out here."

"You think?" I asked sincerely.

She paused her running. Her pretty cheeks were pink and healthy-looking. She'd worn her long hair in a ponytail today, and she wore blue jeans that fit her perfectly.

"Yeah, I do. I think it's time you get your feet wet, rookie. Use the audio recorder. Ask a few questions."

"Um, what? What kind of questions?"

"Ask a question like, 'Are there any spirits around me that want to talk?'"

I repeated what she said. I spun around slowly and looked around the forest, but there wasn't a sound.

Not even bird sounds or a squirrel rattling through the leaves. And it didn't just sound dead; it felt dead.

About *The Ghosts of Kali Oka Road*

The paranormal investigators at Gulf Coast Paranormal thought they knew what they were doing. Midas, Sierra, Sara, Josh and Peter had over twenty combined years of experience investigating supernatural activity on the Gulf Coast. But when they meet Cassidy, a young artist with a strange gift, they realize there's more to learn. And time is running out for Cassidy.

When Gulf Coast Paranormal begins investigating the ghosts of Kali Oka Road, they find an entity far scarier than a few ghosts. Add in the deserted Oak Grove Plantation, and you have a recipe for a night of terror.

More from M. L. Bullock

From *Wife of the Left Hand*

Okay, so it was official. I *had* lost my mind. I turned off the television and got up from the settee. I couldn't explain any of it, and who would believe me? Too many weird things had happened today—ever since I arrived at Sugar Hill.

Just walk away, Avery. Walk away. That had always been good advice, Vertie's advice, actually.

And I did.

I took a long hot bath, slid into some comfortable pinstriped pajamas, pulled my hair into a messy bun and climbed into my king-sized bed.

All was well. Until about midnight.

A shocking noise had me sitting up straight in the bed. It was the loudest, deepest clock I had ever heard, and it took forever for the bells to ring twelve times. After the last ring, I flopped back on my bed and pulled the covers over my head. Would I be able to go back to sleep now?

To my surprise, the clock struck once more. What kind of clock struck thirteen? Immediately my room got cold, the kind of cold that would ice you down to your bones. Wrapping the down comforter around me, I turned on the lamp beside me and huddled in the bed, waiting...for something...

I sat waiting, wishing I were brave enough and warm enough to go relight a fire in my fireplace. It was so cold I could see my breath now. Thank God I hadn't slept nude tonight. Jonah had hated when I wore pajamas to bed. *Screw him!* I willed myself to stop thinking about him. That was all in the past now. He'd made his choice, and I had made mine.

Then I heard the sound for the first time. It was soft at first, like a kitten crying pitifully. Was there a lost cat here? That would be totally possible in this big old house. As the mewing sound drew closer, I could hear much more clearly it was not a kitten but a child. A little girl crying as if her heart were broken. Sliding my feet in my fuzzy white slippers and wrapping the blanket around me tightly, I awkwardly tiptoed to the door to listen. Must be one of the housekeepers' children. Probably cold and lost. I imagined if you wanted to, you could get lost here and never be found. Now her crying mixed with whispers as if she were saying something; she was pleading as if her life depended on it. My heart broke at the sound, but I couldn't bring myself to open the door and actually take a look. Not yet. I scrambled for my iPhone and jogged back to the door to record the sounds. How else would anyone believe me? Too many unbelievable things had happened today. With my phone in one hand, the edge of my blanket in my teeth to keep it in place and my free hand on the doorknob, I readied myself to open the door. I had to see who—or what—was crying in the hallway. I tried to turn the icy cold silver-toned knob, but it wouldn't budge. It was as if someone had locked me in. Who would do such a thing? Surely not Dinah or Edith or one of the other staff?

About *Wife of the Left Hand*

Avery Dufresne had the perfect life: a rock star boy-friend, a high-profile career in the anchor chair on a national news program. Until a serious threat brings her perfect world to a shattering stop. When Avery emerges from the darkness she finds she has a new ability—a supernatural one. Avery returns to Belle Fontaine, Alabama, to claim an inheritance: an old plantation called Sugar Hill. Little does she know that the danger has just begun.

More from M. L. Bullock

From *Guinevere Forever*

Where are you, Arthur?

Oh yes, he was here—somewhere close by. The familiar rhythm, the essence of Arthur was here! I closed my eyes and felt around the room with my mind. I was sure this modern-day Arthur would not have the memories that I had. None of his previous incarnations remembered who they were save one. What would I see in him now? Would it be as Morgan said? Did he look much the same? Perhaps this had been a mistake...but then again, Morgan already knew he was here. There was no need to hide him away from her. Whatever her reasons, she had left him behind tonight.

My vampire's heart surged with hunger, and I dug my fingernails into the palms of my hands to keep myself under control while I searched for him. It had been a mistake to forego my feeding. By tomorrow night, I would be ravenous. There were only seven souls here, and two were outside. One would have thought I would know Arthur immediately, but I was cautious, careful. Uncertain.

Sometime in the last century, Arthur had indeed returned and had known, fully known who he was. I watched him closely because he grew up so near to me, so near to where Camelot once stood. It was as if the Once and Future King had truly returned to drag the world back into the light. That Arthur had the same hazel eyes and the shock of blond hair that young Arthur used to have and that our children had. But that boy, my Arthur returned, unfortunately died from a sudden fever, never knowing who I was and never knowing that I was so nearby. But then again, how could a ten-year-old child ever understand what I wanted to tell him? And when he died I had pledged to never seek out my husband again. To never search. Perhaps it would be better even now that I should turn and look the other way. Even now I should leave and not come back...but then I found him. He sat at the bar, his back turned to me. He wore blue jeans and a dirty t-shirt. He was muscular and tall, and I could sense that his mind was full of worry.

Arthur!

The rest of these minds, the ones that weren't soaked in alcohol or obsessed with some horrible secret, were easy to decipher. As he had been when we were alive together, Arthur was now a complex mess of emotions; he wore his character and his feelings on his shoulders just as he used to wear his armor. He was facing a dilemma, one that I did not fully understand, but just seeing him made me clutch my palms into fists in amazement. *This was my Arthur—just as he had been, handsome and strong and intelligent.* I would know him anywhere, and if I could have, I would have wept. But if I knew him, he would also know me and remember. A sudden fear came over me. My goal had been to come here, to seek him and find him, to make contact with him, but I was not prepared to do so now. Oh, to be this old and still be such a coward. Yet, I could not leave Arthur untouched. I could not allow Morgan to have the last evil word whispered in his ear. With my eyes closed, I spoke his name softly.

"Arthur..."

About *Guinevere Forever*

Guinevere thought that her life was over, that she would spend the rest of her days in a convent or hidden away in Avalon, but she was wrong. Cursed by Morgan LeFay, Queen Guinevere is banished from Avalon and must face the ages alone, hiding in the shadows as a vampire. Through the centuries, she's watched Arthur return again and again, but her love and respect for her husband and king has kept her away.

Until now.

Morgan LeFay has returned with an ominous threat, and once again Guinevere is forced to make an impossible choice, but one she cannot avoid. Supernatural forces are arrayed against the once-powerful queen...can she overcome them and settle an ancient score?

More from M. L. Bullock

From *The Mermaid's Gift*

Dauphin Island had more than its share of weirdness—a fact illustrated by tomorrow's Mullet Toss—but it was home to me. It wasn't as popular as nearby Sand Island or Frenchman Bay, and we islanders clung to our small-town identity like it was a badge of honor. Almost unanimously, islanders refused to succumb to the pressure of beach developers and big-city politicians who occasionally visited our pristine stretches of sand with dollar signs in their eyes. No matter how they sweet-talked the town elders, they left unsatisfied time and time again, with the exception of a lone tower of condominiums that stood awkwardly in the center of the island. As someone said recently at our monthly town meeting, "We don't need all that hoopla." That seemed to be the general sense of things, and although I valued what they were trying to preserve, I didn't always agree with my fellow business owners and residents. Still, I was just Nike Augustine, the girl with a weird name and a love for french fries but most notably the granddaughter of the late Jack Augustine, respected one-time mayor of Dauphin Island. What did I know? I was too young to appreciate the importance of protecting our sheltered island. Or so I had been told. So island folk such as myself made the bulk of our money during spring break and the Deep Sea Fishing Rodeo in July. It was enough to make a girl nuts.

But despite this prime example of narrow-mindedness, I fit in here. Along with all the oddities like the island clock that never worked properly, the abandoned lighthouse that everyone believed was haunted and the fake purple shark that hung outside my grandfather's souvenir shop. I reminded myself of that when the overwhelming desire to wander overtook me, as it threatened to do today and had done most days recently. I had even begun to dream of diving into the ocean and swimming as far down as I could. Pretty crazy since I feared the water, or more specifically what swam hidden in the darkness. Another Nike eccentricity. Only my grandfather understood my reluctance, but he was no longer here to tell me I wasn't crazy. My fear of water separated me from my friends, who practically lived in or on the waters of the Gulf of Mexico or the Mobile Bay most of the year.

Meandering down the aisles of the souvenir shop, I stopped occasionally to turn a glass dolphin and rearrange a few baskets of dusty shells. I halfheartedly slapped the shelves with my dust rag and glanced at the clock again and again until finally the shark-tooth-tipped hands hit five o'clock. With a bored sigh, I walked to the door, turned the sign to Closed and flicked off the neon sign that glowed: "Shipwreck Souvenirs." I'd keep longer hours when spring break began, but for now it was 9 to 5.

I walked to the storeroom to retrieve the straw broom. I had to pay homage to tradition and make a quick pass over the chipped floor. I'd had barely any traffic today, just a few landlubbers hoping to avoid the spring breakers; as many early birds had discovered, the cold Gulf waters weren't warm enough to frolic in yet. Probably fewer than a dozen people had darkened my door today, and only half of those had the courtesy to buy something. With another sigh, I remembered the annoying child who had rubbed his sticky hands all over the inflatables before announcing to the world that he had to pee. I thanked my Lucky Stars that I didn't have kids. But then again, I would need a boyfriend or husband for that, right?

Oh, yeah. I get to clean the toilets, too.

I wondered what the little miscreant had left behind for me in the tiny bathroom. No sense in griping about it. It was me or no one. I wouldn't be hiring any help anytime soon. I grabbed the broom and turned to take care of the task at hand when I heard a suspicious sound that made me pause.

Someone was near the back door, rattling through the garbage cans. I could hear the metal lid banging on the ground. Might be a cat or dog, but it might also be Dauphin Island's latest homeless resident. We had a few, but this lost soul tugged at my heart-strings. I had never seen a woman without a place to live. So far she had refused to tell me her name or speak to me at all. Perhaps she was hard of hearing too? Whatever the case, it sounded as if she weren't above digging through my trash cans. Which meant even more work for me. "Hey," I called through the door, hoping to stop her before she destroyed it.

I had remembered her today as I was eating my lunch. I saved her half of my club sandwich. I had hoped I could tempt her to talk to me, but as if she knew what I had planned, she'd made herself scarce. Until now.

I slung the door open, and the blinds crashed into the mauve-painted wall. Nobody was there, but a torn bag of trash lay on the ground. I yelled in the direction of the cans, "Hey! You don't have to tear up the garbage! I have food for you. Are you hungry?"

I might as well have been talking to the dolphins that splashed offshore. Nobody answered me. "I know you're there! I just heard you in my trash. Come out, lady. I won't hurt you." Still nobody answered. I heard a sound like a low growl coming from the side of my store.

What the heck was that?

Immediately I felt my adrenaline surge. Danger stalked close. I ran to the back wall of my shop and flattened myself against the rough wood. I heard the growl again. Was that a possum? Gator? Rabies-crazed homeless lady? I knew I shouldn't have started binge-watching *The Walking Dead* this week. There was absolutely nothing wrong with my imagination. My mind reeled with the possibilities. After a few seconds I quietly reasoned with myself. I didn't have time for this. Time to face the beast—whatever it might be.

About *The Mermaid's Gift*

Nike Augustine isn't your average girl next door. She's a spunky siren but, thanks to a memory loss, doesn't know it—yet. By day, she runs a souvenir shop on Dauphin Island off the coast of Alabama, but a chance encounter opens her eyes to the supernatural creatures that call the island home, including a mermaid, a fallen goddess and a host of other beings. When an old enemy appears and attempts to breach the Sirens Gate, Nike and her friends must take to the water to prevent the resurrection of a long-dead relative...but the cost might be too high.

To make matters worse, Nike has to choose between longtime crush, Officer Cruise Castille and Ramara, a handsome supernaturate who has proven he's willing to lose everything—including his powers—for the woman he loves.

Read more from M.L. Bullock

The Seven Sisters Series

Seven Sisters
Moonlight Falls on Seven Sisters
Shadows Stir at Seven Sisters
The Stars that Fell
The Stars We Walked Upon
The Sun Rises Over Seven Sisters

The Idlewood Series

The Ghosts of Idlewood
Dreams of Idlewood
The Whispering Saint
The Haunted Child

*Return to Seven Sisters
(A Sequel Series to Seven Sisters)*

The Roses of Mobile
All the Summer Roses

The Gulf Coast Paranormal Series

The Ghosts of Kali Oka Road
The Ghosts of the Crescent Theater
A Haunting at Bloodgood Row
The Legend of the Ghost Queen
A Haunting at Dixie House
The Ghost Lights of Forrest Field

The Sugar Hill Series

Wife of the Left Hand
Fire on the Ramparts
Blood by Candlelight
The Starlight Ball

Ghosts of Summerleigh Series

The Belles of Desire, Mississippi
The Ghost of Jeopardy Belle

Lost Camelot Series

Guinevere Forever

The Desert Queen Series

The Tale of Nefret
The Falcon Rises
The Kingdom of Nefertiti
The Song of the Bee-Eater

The Sirens Gate Series

The Mermaid's Gift
The Blood Feud
The Wrath of Minerva

Standalone books

Ghosts on a Plane

To receive updates on her latest releases,
visit her website at MLBullock.com
and subscribe to her mailing list.

52438586R00129

Made in the USA
Lexington, KY
13 September 2019